THE HAPPY HOLIDATES BOXED SET

S.L. STERLING

POP TARTS AND MISTLETOE

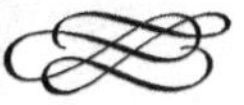

Pop Tarts and Mistletoe

CHAPTER ONE

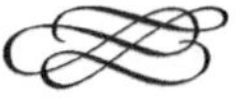

Maya

I made my way down the boarding bridge. It had been a long flight, and I'd never been more ready to disembark a plane than I was right now. It was the worst flight I'd had in the past five years. The turbulence was so bad I'd spent the last hour with a sickness bag in my hands. That hadn't happened since my first flight four years ago.

Being a travel writer had its perks. I got to see amazing parts of the world—parts I probably wouldn't have gotten to see otherwise. I loved Fiji, Hawaii, and Bali, and probably would live in all three if given the chance. However, there were places I'd visited that I hated. Australia, for instance, while beautiful, was home to some of the most venomous creatures ever. While I was in Vanuatu, I experienced both a cyclone and a volcanic eruption. Not something I'd recommend. I wasn't sure which was worse.

Tonight was Christmas Eve-Eve-Eve. It was something silly my brother and I had come up with as kids to count down the nights before Christmas. I was homesick, and I was so close to home I could taste it, and then the plane had to make an emergency landing in Minnesota because of the storm that had hit. As soon as I entered the airport, I made my way over to the attendant at the desk.

"Miss, excuse me. Miss, I need some help." The woman stood with her face in her computer screen, not paying any attention to me. "Miss, did you hear me? I said I could use some help, please."

She turned her cold grey eyes on me and gave me a horrific look. "One moment," she barked, shuffling around some papers, typing more things into the computer before looking up at me. "How can I help?"

"I was en route to Boston. They instructed the plane I was on coming from Tahiti to land here because of a storm or something. I need to know which gate I need to be at so I can catch the new flight to Boston."

"Miss, look around. The FAA has grounded every flight until further notice. There is nothing going in that direction." She picked up the papers on the small desk. "The best thing you can do for yourself right now would be to head over to the customer service desk and see if they can get you a hotel room for the night."

I stood there, mouth agape, and watched as she shoved the handful of papers into her small bag and took off into the crowd without a care.

Irritated, I looked around. Then I noticed the long line of people at the desk she'd pointed to. I let out a sigh, made my way over to the back of the line, and waited.

Sometime later, I let out a yawn as I glanced at my watch. I'd been in line for a little over an hour. My body ached. I was tired, and I had a headache. I wondered if standing in this line was going to get me anywhere or if I should just abandon it now and go buy myself a lottery ticket. From the looks of it, I had a better chance of winning tonight's draw than I did of getting home tonight. I yawned again, just as I heard a woman's voice yell next in line.

"I said next in line."

I turned to look. She'd been talking to me.

I smiled as I approached the counter. "Yes, my flight got re-routed because of the storm, and I need a room for the night."

She chuckled and muttered something under her

breath as she typed furiously into the computer, shaking her head the entire time.

"What's the problem?" I questioned.

"Nothing. Each of you is the same. You expect me to work miracles." Then she shrugged her shoulders and looked at me. "Sorry, looks like we are all out of rooms."

"How can you be all out of rooms?"

"Miss, look around. I lost count of how many flights they have grounded. Everyone here is going to be spending the night at the airport."

"You can't be serious?"

"I can and I am. There are no more rooms available here or at any hotel in the area."

She slapped a closed sign down on the counter, and everyone who was behind me let out a groan. I sighed, took my bags, and made my way over to sit down and figure out what it was I was going to do to get back home.

I quickly sent a message to my parents, and then my stomach let out a huge growl. It had been hours since I'd eaten. In fact, when the turbulence had started on the flight, we were supposed to get drinks and snacks but that had been put on hold. I glanced around. All restaurants in the area were packed. I finally spotted a vending machine over in the corner that still had a few snacks.

I made my way over and studied what remained. A couple of my least favorite chocolate bars were there, followed by the only chips I couldn't eat since I'd made myself sick on them when I was in my teens. They had a ripped bag of trail mix and the worst tasting protein bars I'd ever eaten. Then, as if I hadn't spotted it before, there sat the very last package of pop tarts. I looked at the vending machine and carefully typed in my selection and waved my phone over it to pay, only it didn't beep. Then I noticed a sign that read cash only. I rolled my eyes and pulled my purse around and dug for my wallet. Who carried cash anymore? I didn't even know if I had enough to buy the overpriced package of pop tarts. I searched for my wallet, coming up ten cents short. Panic set in as I searched the bottom of my purse and finally found my last dime. I put the money into the machine and watched as the spiral arm turned, and just when the pop tart was ready to fall, it stopped.

"Dammit," I muttered as I kicked the machine.

I looked at the dangling package, anger filling me. The vending machine gods were mocking me. I could almost hear them laughing as I tried to determine my best method of attack. Kicking, hitting, or shaking the hell out of the vending machine until that packet fell were my only options. I placed my purse at my feet and slid my bag off to the side and was about to shake the machine when someone shoved a microphone in my face.

"Windy Rain reporting from the airport here in

Minnesota where thousands of passengers are stranded because of bad weather. Tell me, how do you feel about being stuck here tonight?"

I looked over to my left to see a large camera pointed in my direction as this Windy Rain person stood there with a dumb-looking smile on her face. *How did I feel about being stuck here? How did she think I felt being stuck here?*

She said nothing, and when I didn't respond, she smiled and said, "How is this delay going to interrupt your holiday plans?"

I looked back to the dangling package of pop tarts hanging in the vending machine and could feel the tension rising to my shoulders and neck.

"Well, Windy, let's see, shall we? My holiday plans? Well, I was trying to get home, to spend the holidays with my family, but that's ruined, and instead I am stuck here. Just like these pop tarts," I said, knocking my fist into the glass door of the vending machine, giving her a death stare. "I was going to eat these for dinner, but like my holidays, c'est la vie. There are no more hotel rooms. I've spent close to twelve hours on a plane already, and I was looking forward to being home in my bed tonight. So, Windy, why don't you tell me how you think I'm doing?"

She pulled the microphone away from my lips, and with a shocked expression, turned back to the camera.

"It appears that just like every holiday traveler here in the airport, tensions are high," she sang into the microphone as she walked away from me, heading toward another unsuspecting person.

"I'll give her *tensions are high*," I mocked as I watched her walk away before turning my attention back to the vending machine in front of me that held my pop tarts hostage.

CHAPTER TWO

Liam

I WATCHED her as I sat at a table near where she stood kicking the crap out of the vending machine. She was cute. She was feisty, and she certainly wasn't afraid to take charge of a situation. She'd handled the reporter with ease. In fact, it had brought a smile to my lips.

I couldn't help but smile when she raised her hands over her head and began doing a dance in front of the vending machine. Then she reached down and pulled a foil pack from the dispensing area. As she approached my table, I took another look at her. Her ponytail swung from side to side. She looked comfy in a pair of black yoga pants and a sweatshirt, and now that she had food in her hands, she looked a little more relaxed.

She stopped just beside my table and looked around the enormous area, defeat settling on her face. There had been nowhere to sit for hours. I'd watched people come and go. She spun around, looking behind her, and when she thought she'd found a spot, she left, only to stop when someone else sat down in it.

"You can sit here if you like," I said loud enough for her to hear.

She glanced over at me as I nodded to the empty seat across from me. "There aren't many tables left, and at least these seats are cushy."

She smiled cautiously, and then looked around.

"Are you speaking to me?" she questioned.

"I am. Take a seat. I promise I won't touch your pop tarts," I said, nodding to the package in her hand.

Her cheeks reddened. "Oh god, you saw all that didn't you?"

"I did. I will say I have never seen someone so determined to get a package of pop tarts before."

She laughed, then wheeled her bags over and placed them under the edge of the table beside mine and slid into the booth. "In my defense, they were the only thing in there that I liked."

"Hey, there's no judgment on my part. I just found it amusing. I'm Liam."

"Maya." She smiled, ripping open the package of pop tarts and sliding one out of the package, taking a bite.

An employee from the little cafe across the way came over with a tray of eggnog. "Can I offer you each one?" the lady asked.

I glanced at Maya and each of us nodded. The lady placed two small glasses of eggnog down on the table then continued to the next table.

"Eggnog without rum. I don't know how I'll be able to get it down," she mumbled to herself, looking at the small glass.

I reached into my bag and removed two small bottles of rum I'd been saving for my flight. I hated flying, and downing two of these small bottles before getting on the plane were normally enough to take the edge off. I shoved one across the table to Maya, and as soon as she saw it, she smiled.

"Nothing like eggnog and rum." I smiled.

She slowly reached for the bottle, but before she opened it, she slid the package of pop tarts to me and smiled. "Thank you."

"Hey, I'm not taking your other pop tart. I don't need you taking out your aggression on me like you did that machine over there." I winked.

"I insist," she said, cracking the small bottle of rum open and dumping the contents into the eggnog, stirring it with her finger before taking a sip, while I did the same. "After all, you saved me from having to drink this thimble of eggnog down."

I chuckled. "Where were you headed?" I questioned, pulling the pop tart from the package and breaking it in half.

"I'm a travel writer. I was on my way back from Bora Bora, heading home to Boston for the holidays. What about you?"

"Wow! You travel all alone?"

"I do."

"Huh, I would have thought you'd have had someone with you."

"Someone as in a guy?" she questioned, taking a drink of her eggnog.

"Perhaps." I shrugged.

Maya leaned forward and looked me in the eyes. "Liam, do I look helpless to you?"

I swallowed hard and shook my head. "You, um, you seem very capable. I didn't mean it to insult you."

Maya laughed. "That's what growing up with JJ will do. He tortured me regularly. Ever since then, everything seems easier, even deciding when to leave," she said, reaching across and breaking off half of the pop tart that was left and shoving it back over to me.

"Over JJ?" I questioned.

"No, over Matt."

Confused now, I looked at her. "Matt is another brother?"

"JJ is my brother. Matt is my ex. I thought we were forever. He thought we were… for now."

"Ah, I see."

"Yep. It was a Christmas surprise from hell," She said, rolling her eyes and making a funny face.

"Dare I ask?" I chuckled at her expression.

"Oh, you know. Just another Christmas gone wrong. I came home for Christmas break from school. I was in my senior year at college to find he'd brought a girl home to meet the family. He played it off as if she were just a friend without a place to go for the holidays, but then I found out that he proposed."

"Oh, come on. Seriously?"

Maya nodded her head and shoved a piece of pop tart in her mouth. "Not kidding. His excuse was the distance was killing him. So, I swallowed my hurt and the fact that he cheated on me, and at the end of senior year, I focused on me. So, I applied for jobs everywhere but Boston."

"So, you ran away?"

She looked at me and shook her head. "No. I took control of a situation that I had no control over, and I've been doing it ever since."

"Otherwise known as running away." I winked.

She let out a huff and then smiled. "God, you sound

like JJ." She rolled her eyes and took another bite of her pop tart. "Now, what is your story? What are you running away from?" she said, smiling.

"Well, I'm with the military, and I'm headed to be with my best friend for the holidays. I've spent the last five years with Whitty, and I see no reason to break tradition."

Maya nodded. "So, this Whitty, how did you meet?"

"Through work. He was in the military for a bit with me and we just seemed to hit it off. Once he left, our paths ended up crossing a few more times that first year. I was back in Boston five years ago at Christmas to teach a course and ran into Whitty. He was taking the course I was teaching, and he invited me to stay with him and his family for the holidays. So, I took him up on the offer and spent the holidays there instead of at the hotel alone, and now it's a holiday tradition."

"That was really nice of him."

I nodded. "Yep. We've had a lot of adventures together over the past five years, but most of all, he's like the brother I never had."

"What about your family?"

I shook my head. "My family is my military family. Otherwise, I have none. I do not know who my parents are. I was in and out of foster care until I was eighteen. In and out of more homes than I can count."

"Oh. I'm sorry."

"Don't be. It doesn't bother me to talk about it."

"So, this Whitty, he's like the brother you never had?"

"Yeah, he's quite the guy. I'm lucky to have him and his family, to be honest. They welcomed me in with open arms."

"Wow sounds like a special friendship. I'd love to meet him and hear about all your adventures. It's probably my favorite part of my job, getting to know people."

"Well, I'd love to meet the guy responsible for making you so tough." I winked. "I don't know how comfortable I'd be having my sister travel the world alone."

"It comes with its fair share of danger, but you soon gather a sense of who you can trust and who you can't."

I smiled. "Well, I hope I don't give you those danger vibes," I said, winking.

She was beautiful when she smiled. I could barely take my eyes off her, and when she lifted those blue eyes of hers to mine, I prayed I didn't appear as some creep. "Just the opposite. Right from the second you invited me to sit with you, I knew I was in good company."

"Good, I'm glad."

We talked well into the night. We even shared a basket of fries and more stories, allowing the time we had to wait to pass quickly. I was about to point out that the sun was rising when a woman screamed, causing us both to jump. We looked over and saw a bunch of people gathered at the large window.

"Look! A plow!" one man exclaimed.

"Looks like they are clearing the loading area," another lady replied.

"Looks like we may get our holiday wishes after all," another lady cried as she hugged her daughter.

Maya turned and looked at me, smiling. "Looks like we both may get our wish after all."

I nodded and smiled and was about to say something when the overhead speaker came on, directing people to check in with airport staff. Once the announcement had been made, I looked over at Maya.

"Thank you for the company. It was wonderful to get to spend the evening with someone."

Maya had already slipped out of the booth and gathered her stuff, slinging her purse over her shoulder and was about to walk away.

"Wait. I just wanted to thank you. It was nice. However, I don't think you need to rush. We can always head to the counter together. We are heading in the same direction, after all."

"That is true," Maya said, smiling. "To be honest, I'd love nothing more than more of your company."

I slid from the booth and gathered my things, and together we made our way over to one of the airport employees.

CHAPTER THREE

Maya

I SHOVED my suitcase in the overhead bin, slipped my sweater on, and sat down in my seat. Turned out that Liam and I were on the same flight, so we requested we sit next to one another. I secured my seat belt then looked at Liam, who sat there looking pale.

"It sure is luck we ended up on the same flight, huh?" he said, swallowing hard.

I could see a light sheen of sweat on his forehead, and I noticed he was clenching the armrest tightly.

"Are you okay? You look a little nervous."

He gave me an awkward smile and swallowed hard. "Nervous flyer…"

I couldn't help but giggle. "Um…Liam…how the hell did you jump out of a plane and off a bridge if you are a nervous flyer?"

"Those two things are completely unrelated."

I couldn't help but laugh. "No, they aren't. The only difference is that you are jumping out of the plane. Please tell me you'd rather be safe in one than jump out of one?"

"Can't say that I would, to be honest. I'll be okay. I normally take a couple of shots before I fly, just enough to take the edge off." He smiled crookedly at me.

It was then I realized he had given me one of those tiny bottles of rum, which I knew for a fact he was probably saving for this flight. I adjusted my sweatshirt, then held out my hand for him to take.

"Oh gosh, you don't need to hold my hand. I'll be fine," Liam said, still gripping each armrest tightly.

"I do. I would like to use the armrest as well, and this seems to be the only way I'll get to." I softly smiled.

He slid his large hand into mine and closed his eyes while steadying his breathing while we taxied out to the runway. Soon we were in the air, and Liam had still not let go of my hand.

The plane was quiet, and once we'd had a drink and a snack, we both reclined our seats back. I opened my eyes when I felt Liam squeeze my hand tight. I lifted my head and placed it back down to find a wet spot on his shoulder. Embarrassment flooded me as I pulled my hand from his and used the hood of my sweatshirt to wipe the drool from the side of my face. I wanted to die. I'd drooled on his shoulder.

"We are just about to land," Liam whispered.

I couldn't even face him, but he grabbed my hand. "It's okay. I don't care that you drooled on me." He winked.

I wanted to die. I leaned back against my seat; I never wanted to look at him again, and as soon as we said goodbye after we landed, that was exactly what I planned on doing.

"My brother is supposed to be here to pick me up," I said, searching for him in the crowd of people. "I just don't see him anywhere."

"Well, Maya, it was a pleasure. I need to grab my luggage and then go meet Whitty."

"Thank you for everything. It was nice to spend time with someone. It helped ease some of the holiday travel stress." I smiled.

"My pleasure. It's not every day I get to spend time with a cutie like you. Especially one who drools on my shoulder. Anyway, keep being feisty, and I look forward to reading your travel blog."

I'd given him the name of my blog while on the plane. He said he had been wanting to visit Vanuatu, and I told him I was sure I could change his mind.

"I'll also keep my eyes peeled for your blog about your flight home. Just make sure that you don't name me something silly."

I smiled. "I promise I won't."

"Oh, but make sure you keep the part about the drool. It was my favorite." He winked.

I could feel embarrassment flood my cheeks as he smiled at me.

"Merry Christmas, Maya. Safe travels to wherever your next adventure leads."

He gave me one last smile and then Liam disappeared into the crowd. As he walked away from me, I noticed just how big and muscular he was and imagined what it would have been like to be held by that man. One could dream, I thought to myself, and let out a deep sigh. There was no use in wishing for it because I knew that a relationship wasn't in the cards for me. Instead, I turned to the two large doors on my right and pushed them open. Immediately, I began searching the crowd for my brother. Finally, I spotted him leaning against the coffee shop counter, checking his phone for messages.

I walked over to where he was. "Well, well. Hey, JJ."

"Maya! It's about time. I was getting worried."

I waved his worry away with a swipe of my hand. "Tell me about it. Sorry to be late," I said, wrapping arms around his neck and giving him a hug. "What do you say we get out of here? I am exhausted."

JJ glanced at his watch. "I'd love to. You know how I hate having my sleep interrupted, but I'm also waiting for a buddy of mine."

"What? You said nothing about a friend of yours. Nor did Mom."

"Well, your flights were coming in close to the same time. He shouldn't be too long. He sent me a message a bit ago, letting me know he just needed to get his luggage."

"It's fine. I just want to get out of this airport. I've just spent a lot of time with strangers this holiday and was looking forward to spending time with nothing but family. Now I guess I'll be spending it with strangers at home as well."

JJ chuckled. "Don't worry, it will be like having another big brother. Instead of only needing to put up with me, you'll have to put up with me and another one." He winked.

I glanced over my shoulder and spotted a sign for a

women's washroom. If I had to wait, I needed to use the washroom. I cleared my throat. "Look, leave without me, and I'm telling Mom. I just need to use the little girls' room. Be useful and buy me a coffee, would you?"

"If I do that, then we will need to stop on the way home!" JJ yelled as I walked away. I couldn't help but laugh. It was good to be home.

Twenty minutes later, I made my way back through the crowd. The line had been torturous for someone who'd had to go for a while. I shoved my way through the people and spotted my brother still standing in the same spot, now speaking to someone who had their back to me. At least now we'd be able to get going, I thought to myself.

I walked over and grabbed the cup that sat beside my brother's, paying no attention to the guy he was speaking to. I grabbed the handle of my suitcase, certain that they'd be ready to run out of there, when my brother tapped me on the shoulder.

"What?"

"Maya, I'd like you to meet Tank."

I stood up, a look of shock lining my face, I was sure. The nickname suited him, and I knew my cheeks were on fire as I stood there staring at Liam.

Instead of greeting me, he smiled. "Here you were worried you'd never see me again."

I glanced at my brother. I could tell he wondered

what the hell he was talking about. I stood there ready to die because all I could think about was the puddle of drool I'd left on his shoulder.

"You two know one another?"

I nodded as Liam filled my brother in while we made our way to the car.

CHAPTER FOUR

Liam

I GRABBED the remote and flipped the channel, rolling onto my side as my stomach let out a large growl. I glanced at the clock beside the bed. I'd been in bed almost two hours and still hadn't fallen asleep. Joe and I had been the last to go to bed. First had been Andy and Marlene, Joe's parents, and shortly after that, Maya had turned in.

My stomach let out another growl, and I kicked the covers off. I needed something in my stomach, or I'd never get to bed. I'd barely eaten anything at dinner, and I knew I'd pay for it. I knew Marlene had wrapped and put away the rest of the apple pie, and it was calling my name.

Quietly, I climbed the stairs from the basement and made my way through the dark house to the kitchen. Pulling open the fridge door, I grabbed a small plate from the cupboard and pulled the pie out of the fridge. I cut myself a piece and shoved it onto the plate, wrapping the rest of the pie back up and shoving it back in the fridge. I then grabbed a glass and filled it halfway full of milk.

I closed the fridge door, turned around to take a seat at the breakfast bar, and jumped. Standing there, quiet as a mouse in the shadows, was Maya.

"Sorry, I didn't mean to scare you," she whispered, stepping into the kitchen and flipping the light on over the stove before reaching for a glass in the cupboard.

"It's okay. I wasn't exactly expecting anyone to be up." I chuckled.

"I was thirsty." She turned the water on and filled up her glass.

My eyes ran down the length of her body. She looked adorably sexy in a tight tank top and baby doll shorts. My eyes lingered on her perfectly round ass. I swallowed hard. I'd found her attractive at the airport, but this was different. She cleared her throat, and I tore my eyes away from her. Had she known I'd been watching her the entire time? Had she seen my lingering gaze? When I looked at her, I realized the pink hue on her cheeks in the dim light. Only she wasn't looking at my face. Instead, her eyes were fixed on my shirtless chest.

She picked up her glass and placed it in front of the seat she sat down on at the breakfast bar, while I did the same. We sat there in quiet, me eating and her drinking, saying nothing to one another. Then she cleared her throat as she watched me lift a forkful of pie to my mouth.

"I really need to apologize to you about the drool. It mortified me when I turned around and saw that you were…"

I chuckled. "Maya, seriously, please don't worry about it," I said, digging my fork into the pie once again. "Or should I say, Booger?"

Maya buried her face in her hands. She'd just about killed Joe when he'd called her that in the car on the way home. I couldn't help but laugh at first, sort of like now as I thought about it, but I was curious where that nickname had come from.

"I swear, I'm going to kill him," she mumbled, scrunching her nose and making an adorable face.

"Care to tell me how you got that nickname?" I asked, leaning in and bumping her shoulder.

She sighed. "Must I?"

I got up off the stool, went around to the fridge, and

pulled out the pie again, this time grabbing another plate from the cupboard. I cut another sliver of pie for myself and one for her, and then I dug into the freezer.

"What are you doing?"

"Well, from how red your face is, I can tell this must be a whopper of a story. So, pie and ice cream it is." I stood up, holding the vanilla ice cream container, and winked.

She rolled her eyes first, but then finally smiled as she watched while I completed both plates.

"Now tell me all about it," I said, placing her plate in front of her and handing her a fork while I carried mine around and sat back down beside her.

I watched as she slid the fork into her pie and slid the delicious, sweet dessert past her lips, a soft smile resting on them.

"I swear to god, you breathe a word of this to anyone and we are going to have a problem."

"Is that so?"

She looked at me and nodded. "It is."

"You think you could take me on?" I questioned.

She ran her eyes over me and nodded. "Definitely. You don't look so tough."

I chuckled. "My dear, I'm tougher than you think."

"Not true. You have weak spots just like the next guy, and JJ taught me all about them. So, don't test me." She giggled.

I dug my fork into my pie and looked at her. "Okay then. If that is the case, I swear on this pie."

She squinted her eyes as she looked at me in disbelief. "You swear on this pie?" she mimicked. "How am I supposed to trust that? Sounds like something Joe would say while trying to get me to confess something he wanted to know?"

My jaw dropped, and I shook my head. "I swear on this pie because it is the best damn pie I've ever had."

"Oh please. You didn't think I'd fall for that?"

I frowned. "I'm not trying to get you to fall for anything. I mean it," I said, my expression turning serious at the fact she'd think I'd lie to get her to tell me something.

"Yeah okay. Whatever." She laughed.

I didn't find it funny. I was being serious with her, but the more times she looked over at me to find a serious look on my face, it only made her laugh harder. Instead of saying anything, I turned back to my plate and finished the dessert. Then I got up and placed the plate in the sink and emptied the glass of milk. When I finally placed the glass in the sink, she'd stopped laughing.

"Where are you going?" she questioned.

"To bed. It's clear you think I was only trying to get the story out of you to embarrass you, so I'd prefer you don't tell me. Good night, Maya."

I'd just grabbed hold of the doorknob leading back to

the basement when I felt her small, warm hand on my shoulder.

"Wait, I'm sorry. I didn't mean to laugh at what you said. It's just I'm used to Joe tricking me. He used to do these things to get me to tell him things so that he could make fun of me. I thought you were doing the same thing."

"I get it, but I'm not like that. I was seriously interested to know how a pretty girl like yourself got the nickname booger."

She looked into my eyes and slid her hand in mine and led me over to the couch. As we walked, my eyes fell to her ass. I shouldn't be looking at her like this. Joe would kill me. But she really was sexy as hell. So sexy, in fact, that I wished Joe had invoked the bro code when he knew she was going to be staying here.

She sat down on the corner of the couch and pulled one of the small square cushions to her chest, covering herself from my wandering eyes.

"Okay, I was about fourteen. I'd come home from a run and went into the kitchen to get a snack and a drink. While there, Joe came in with one of his best friends, Paul. Paul was captain of our school's baseball team and had the dreamiest blue eyes, like yours, and I had the biggest crush on him. Anyway, I stood there gushing over Paul, telling him story after story just to keep him in the room, while Joe stood behind him, wiping at his nose."

"Oh, no. I can see where this is going."

"Yeah, well, I ignored him and stood there and talked to the guy I was crushing on with a… oh god… it was mortifying."

"So that is why you got the nickname?"

"Not even close. They'd just heated their dinner. They both sat down, and Paul took the pepper grinder and began putting pepper over his food. The window was open, and I caught a whiff of the pepper and I sneezed, launching that wonderful little friend of mine right onto Paul's plate."

I couldn't help but laugh. "No, you didn't."

"Oh, I did. Paul took one look and began gagging, and well, I took off to my room wishing I could just die of embarrassment."

"And so he gave you that nickname?" I chuckled.

Maya nodded. "The most embarrassing moment of my teen years, and he immortalized it with that stupid nickname."

"So does that mean I can't call you booger?" I asked, smiling.

"That is exactly what it means."

"Well, it seems you both have something in common."

"What would that be?"

"Snot rockets!" I smiled.

"Oh god, please tell me he still isn't doing that?"

I chuckled. "Not since he got punished in the military for that. To my knowledge, that was the last time. Thank you for trusting me with that story."

"Well, if I find it makes the rounds, or it suddenly comes up at dinner, I'll make it my mission to make sure you have no more pie."

As we sat there laughing, our eyes met, and soon we just sat there in silence, looking at one another. I finally leaned back and closed my eyes for a minute, just taking in the silence. I was grateful for it.

I felt her warm hand on my knee. "I noticed you didn't eat much at dinner."

I opened my eyes and met her gaze while shaking my head. "No, there was just a lot of noise and too many people here tonight. Not something I was expecting after the airport. It's sometimes hard for me to settle into large crowds."

She nodded. "You sound like JJ. You have PTSD as well?"

I could tell from the look on her face she meant what she was asking. Joe had suffered terribly once he'd left the military. We talked about it, and we shared stories. I nodded. "There aren't many of us that don't. Joe just hides it better than I do."

"I don't think he does. I do know that he packs lighter than you." She winked.

I chuckled. "Now don't go picking on a guy with PTSD about his packing habits." I chuckled. "Actually, I'm moving here. I called Joe ahead of time. Most of my stuff is in a storage locker that Joe arranged. He asked your parents if I could stay here until I find a place of my own."

"Makes sense to me now why they gave you the basement instead of the spare room across from mine."

I'd known about that room, having stayed in it the prior times I'd been here. I figured perhaps it was Maya's room, and that was why they'd given me the basement.

She glanced at the clock on the wall, then smiled at me and stood up. I watched as she made her way to the kitchen and began putting things into the dishwasher. I got up and followed, watching her every move. Once she'd finished, she softly smiled at me. "Good night."

I smiled and allowed her to come around the counter, then followed her over toward the basement door.

"I'll see you in the morning," she whispered, then glanced up toward the ceiling, a small smile coming to her lips as a soft-pink hue landed on her cheeks.

"What?"

She lifted her eyes toward the ceiling and back at me. I too glanced up and noticed the small green bunch of mistletoe hanging above our heads. I brought my hand to her cheek and met her gaze. The world seemed to stop as I slowly leaned in and grazed her lips. The second I felt her hand on my chest, I gripped her hip with my free hand and kissed her harder. It had been something I'd been dying to do since I'd laid eyes on her.

CHAPTER FIVE

Maya

I WAS JUST ABOUT to take a bite of my pumpkin pie when I felt a foot brush against mine. He'd been doing it throughout dinner. I waited until everyone was back into conversation before meeting Liam's gaze. He sat there, holding a forkful of pumpkin pie while giving me a playful look.

"Did you hear what I said, booger?" Joe asked from across the table.

I glanced over to see he was watching me. "What?"

"I asked you if you knew who moved back into town?"

I dropped my eyes back down to my pie while still

feeling Liam's foot rubbing against mine and shook my head while trying to figure out who it could be. "I don't know."

I knew who I didn't want it to be, and that was Matt. I'd never wanted to lay eyes on him again after what he'd done. If it was him, I already knew that having him back in town would mean I'd probably run into him tonight at the festival. It would also ultimately ruin the first Christmas I'd had back home with my family in five years.

"Matt and his new wife."

The table grew quiet, and I could feel all eyes on me as the words sunk into my mind. I took a minute, drawing little designs on the top of my pie with my fork while I tried to digest what Joe had just said. The silence was getting to me, and I slowly lifted my eyes, first to meet Liam's and then to meet Joe's and then both of my parents'.

"Joe, what is the matter with you. Why would you say that to her?"

"She has a right to know, Mom." Joe shrugged. "Besides, I'd rather tell her before we go to the festival tonight and we run into him with her. Just trying to give booger some warning."

"That's enough, Joe," my father replied. "Although, Marlene, I think he may have a point. The last thing we want is for Maya to be blindsided."

Blindsided was right. Although a part of me would rather have been blindsided than to have them all sit here talking about me as if I weren't in the room. That wasn't fair.

"Well, you know he will be there, Mom. I am just trying to look out for her."

"Everyone, please stop," I said, raising my voice over their chatter.

Everyone stopped speaking as eyes landed on me.

"You don't need to look out for me. I am a grown woman. Besides, you also don't have to worry about me running into Matt, because I'm not going to the festival."

"Maya, I refuse to let you stay home. It's Christmas, and we want you with the family," Mom stated. "Matt isn't a reason to stay home."

"Well, you can refuse, and yes, it is Christmas. However, I decided that tonight I'm not going. So, all of you enjoy the festival," I said, sliding my chair away from the table, getting up and heading upstairs.

I could already hear them talk as I climbed the stairs, but I didn't care. I slammed my door shut and sat down on the edge of my bed. It didn't matter how long it had been, I still wasn't over his actions. No matter how long I'd been gone, he'd hurt me bad. So bad, in fact, I'd struggled for the past five years of my life with relationships because he'd made me feel I wasn't good enough, not only for him, but for everyone else. My brother hadn't known that because every time he'd asked me if I was seeing someone, I'd fabricate a man. It was easier than telling him why I wasn't seeing someone.

At first, it had been hard lying to him, but it got easier and easier each time I did it, then two or three months later we'd break up. I'd become a natural at making up these relationships. They never asked to meet them because they knew I wasn't ever with them long enough to bring them around.

I got up and wandered over to my window bench and sat down. I used to sit here every night during the Christmas season, normally with a book in hand. When I would take a break I would look out over the street and take in everyone's Christmas lights. I leaned against the window frame and pulled my favorite pillow into my lap. Then the tears I'd been fighting so hard to hide finally slid down my cheeks.

I could hear everyone getting ready downstairs and couldn't wait until I had the house all to myself. I needed space and time to process what Joe had told me. Why Matt being back mattered so much to me I didn't know. I just knew I needed time to be alone.

When I saw my parents make their way to the car, followed by Joe, I got up from where I was sitting and grabbed my sweatshirt and my book. The house would be quiet. When I heard the front door slam, I pulled open my bedroom door and almost screamed when I came face-to-face with Liam.

"Hey," he said, his voice low.

"What are you still doing here? I thought you all left."

"Can we talk?"

"About?"

"About what happened at dinner?"

I shook my head. "There isn't anything to talk about." I went to turn away, but he grabbed my arm and spun me back around.

"Are you really that afraid of running into this guy tonight that you are going to avoid a family tradition?"

I nodded. "I am."

"What happened to the girl who took control of things when she couldn't control them?" he asked, coming into my bedroom and closing the door.

I shrugged. "I guess, it's easier to control when you aren't staring into someone's face."

He took the book and sweater from my hands and placed them down on my bed then took my hands in his. "True, but this doesn't sound like the shit disturber and fighter that I met only a couple of days ago."

I tried to pull away from his grip and walk away, but he wouldn't let me go. Instead, he held on tight, and when I lowered my gaze to the floor, he placed his finger on my chin and raised my head back up.

"What?"

"Your parents want you to go tonight. In fact, they are sitting down in the car right now, waiting."

"Did they send you up here?"

"No, they think I ran downstairs to grab a sweater and hat. I did this on my own," he said, looking proud of himself. "See, when I saw the look on your mom's face when you left the table, I decided I wanted to do something for her."

I frowned. "What does the look on my mother's face have to do with you being up here?"

"Maya, I don't dwell on my past, because it's my past, and the only thing we should ever look at and focus on is our future. Don't let this jackoff stop you from enjoying a night with your family. I know that tonight means a lot to your mom and that you not wanting to go tonight hurts her. You are home for Christmas for the first time in years, and you should enjoy it and not put your focus on some ass who couldn't see your value."

"Liam, you do not know the hurt he caused me."

"I can only imagine, but I can tell you this: not going tonight, not facing him, only lets him continue to have that hold over you. Show him you aren't still hung up on what he did. Show him you have taken control. Take control of the situation."

"But I haven't. I've been hiding out for the better part

of five years, making up boyfriends and burying the hurt."

Liam said nothing; he just stood there watching me. Then he cleared his throat. "Would it make you feel better if you didn't have to make up a boyfriend this time?"

"Liam, what are you talking about?"

"Well, I'm not from around here. So, if it makes you feel better, and for the sake of the occasion, if we ran into him, would it be okay if I had your back?"

I looked at Liam; I felt confused. I wasn't sure what it was he was trying to get at. "What is that supposed to mean?"

"Well, if he is there and begins giving you a hard time, I could always step in as your boyfriend."

I could tell from the tension in his body and jaw that he was nervous at bringing up this idea, and I almost melted instantly. This was the sweetest offer any man had ever made me, and I softly smiled.

"You'd do that?"

"I would. Does this mean you will join us?"

I looked around my room. I'd come home to be with my family, not stay here all alone. I nodded my head, grabbed my sweater off the end of my bed, and followed Liam out of the room.

CHAPTER SIX

Liam

WE'D GONE AROUND MOST of the festival, and the five of us were now standing in line at a small coffee shop. I was deep in conversation with Joe when I felt Maya tap my shoulder.

"What is it?" I questioned.

"Look, they still have the horse-drawn sleigh rides running through the holiday village."

Joe chuckled. "Used to be boogers' favorite thing to do here. It got so bad we'd have to take turns taking her each year."

"God, would you stop calling me that?" Maya said, punching her brother's arm, causing him to laugh.

"Never!" Joe laughed.

"Would you want to go on a sleigh ride?" I questioned, seeing the look in her eye as she looked over toward the small lineup that was now forming.

She nodded. "It really did used to be my favorite part of the festival."

Joe chuckled. "Be forewarned. She used to cry the entire time because she was afraid of the horses."

"That was when I was three."

I couldn't help but laugh. "We will be back," I said, punching Joe in the other arm. "Order us something yummy."

"Are you having a good time?" I asked as we got into the small lineup.

"I am. I'm glad you talked me into coming after all. Here I was so worried about the evening being ruined, and honestly, there was nothing to worry about at all. I should have known better."

"Our insecurities and hurt have a way of doing that to us." I pulled my phone out of my pocket to check the incoming text message.

"Your brother wants to know what you want to drink? Hot chocolate, mint hot chocolate, or coffee? Also, if you want anything to eat?"

I'd finished texting my order and glanced at Maya when she hadn't answered me. Immediately, I took in her pale complexion and worried at expression on her face. I looked around and then back at Maya.

"What is it?" I asked, stepping a little closer to her.

She quickly wiped her eyes with her hand. "It's them," she whispered, still not looking at me.

I quickly texted Joe back and told him to get her a mint hot chocolate with extra marshmallows and the same cranberry scone I'd ordered. Then I shoved my phone into my pocket and turned my attention back to her. She still wasn't looking my way. Instead, her eyes were glued to them.

"Hey," I whispered, taking her hand in mine. "Look at me."

She finally pulled her gaze from them and looked up at me.

"You are okay. I'm here," I whispered.

She nodded her head, her eyes full of tears. "I'm okay. I'm okay," she kept muttering under her breath. "They are approaching," she said through clenched teeth.

Since there was no one behind us now, I knew they were going to line up right behind us. I'd also done a quick count of the couples in line. It looked like we may even share the same sleigh together. I knew she was panicking. I could see her chest rising and falling in rapid succession through her coat. Knowing I needed to do something, I stepped in toward her, brought my thumb and forefinger to her chin, and tilted her head up and lowered my lips to hers. Soon my hand cupped her cheek, the other was around her waist, and my tongue parted her lips.

Everything fell away—the noise in the background, the people, the fact that her brother was probably watching every move I'd made, and for an instant, it was only us. As we parted, our eyes met, and soon everything came flooding back.

"Maya?" a voice said from behind me.

Her eyes left mine, and she looked past me. "Matt?"

Her voice was strained as she wrapped her arm around my waist and leaned into me as if I were the only thing supporting her now.

"How have you been? This is—"

Only she stopped him before he could continue. "Francine. I remember. This is Liam."

I gave him a nod. Normally, I'd shake hands, but there was nothing worthy enough about this guy to even bother. He hadn't even had big enough balls to tell her they were over before he'd brought another woman into the picture. That had made me angry, but seeing him, seeing how upset she was over this jackass, pissed me off even more.

"So, how have you been? When did you get back to town?" he questioned.

I wrapped my arm around her, pulling her in close.

"We've been well," I intercepted, trying to take the pressure off Maya. "We came into town a couple of days ago. We are here spending Christmas with Maya's family."

Matt looked at me and then at Maya. "How long have you guys been together?" he asked, as if he still had some right to claim her.

"Been what now, sweetie, three years together?"

Maya looked up at me. I could see a hint of shock in her eyes, but I quickly gave her a tiny squeeze, letting her know to relax and follow my lead.

"Yes."

"I can't believe it's been that long, to be honest. Seems like only yesterday I met you in that little café in Paris." I gave her waist another little squeeze.

She swallowed hard and met my gaze. "I remember it like it was yesterday. You stood there in your uniform, looking handsome as ever."

I leaned in and kissed her lips. It was the only thing I could do to help take her mind off the situation. As soon as our lips parted Matt cleared his throat.

"What are you up to these days?" he questioned.

Maya surprised me by answering this time. "I'm a travel writer, and Liam is in the military."

"Oh, a military man," Matt said, giving me a once-over. "Never thought Maya would be the type to fall for a guy who's on the road a lot."

I felt Maya squeeze my side as those words fell from

his lips. I glanced over at her to see what I was sure was pain and hurt in her eyes.

"Why would that be, Matt? She's on the road as much as I am."

"Oh, you know. She was just super clingy when we dated. Always calling, always wanting my attention, always questioning where I was. Blah…blah…blah…It was worse once I went away to school."

I felt tension building in my shoulders. I knew what he was doing, and I would not allow it. He would not stand here and put the blame on her for what he'd done. "Well, like I always say, question when something feels wrong. Obviously, your actions must have made her react that way," I finished, looking him directly in the eye.

Maya placed her free hand on my arm and squeezed, then leaned in and whispered to me to let it go, only I couldn't. This guy had once had a wonderful girl on his arm, and he'd treated her like shit. He deserved to know what he did had been wrong.

"What is that supposed to mean?" Matt questioned. "She's an insecure nightmare."

His wife gripped his arm, leaned in, and whispered something to him, but he shoved her off him.

"Sir, will the four of you be going in the same sleigh?" the man who was busy setting everyone up for their sleigh ride questioned.

My eyes stayed glued to Matt's. "No, we will take one on our own," I replied.

"Seriously, look at her. She's glued to you. It's pathetic."

I gripped her tightly against my side. "Well, Matt, glued to my side is exactly where I want her to be. You see, I don't care because I want everyone to know exactly what I have. I want other men to be jealous. I want other men to wish they had what I had. I'd worry if she didn't want to be like this with me."

"Sir, your sleigh is here."

I helped Maya climb up the step, and then I turned to Matt. "I don't feel bad for guys like you. What I feel sorry for is the women you are in a relationship with. Miss, open your eyes and look at what kind of man you are with. I don't know you, but I'm going to hedge a guess you deserve better."

I didn't wait for Matt to speak. Instead, I climbed up into the sleigh and sat down beside Maya, wrapping my arm around her and pulling her into me. Minutes later, we'd pulled away and were on the way away from Matt and the poor girl he called his wife.

WE'D BEEN on this sleigh ride for almost twenty minutes and were now deep in a beautifully lit forest. I was enjoying the quiet sound of the horses' hooves on the pavement while holding Maya by my side. I couldn't have asked for a better way to spend the evening. I'd just adjusted my arm around her when she cleared her throat.

"I just wanted to thank you," Maya said.

"For what?" I questioned.

"For all of that. You didn't need to stand up for me."

"Isn't that what all fake boyfriends do?" I questioned.

Maya lifted her head from where it was resting on my shoulder and softly smiled. "When you offered to step in as my fake boyfriend, I didn't expect you to take the role so seriously."

I shrugged. "I'm sorry, but the guy is a dick. He deserved so much more than what I'd given him."

"I know. I'd known it for a long time. I was just surprised at the things you said."

I frowned. "You were. Why is that?"

"Because I've never known a man to like to be clung to." She shrugged.

Our eyes locked and we sat there in the quietness, soft Christmas music playing from the small speaker that was attached to the sleigh.

"I say things that are true. I meant what I said, that if you were mine, that glued to my side was where I'd want you to be. He didn't realize what he had when he had you."

A tear slipped down her cheek. I sat up, brought my hand to her cheek, and wiped the tear away with my thumb. With tear-filled eyes, she studied me. I wasn't giving her another chance to doubt what I'd said. I leaned in and kissed her lips.

CHAPTER SEVEN

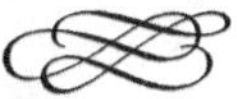

Maya

THE SOFT GLOW of the outdoor Christmas lights lit up my room as I lay in bed, staring up at the ceiling. We'd done a ton of boxing day shopping today, but despite being tired, I'd been lying here for a little over two hours tossing and turning. The only thing on my mind had been what happened last night at the festival.

It wasn't so much what he'd said to Matt, but what had happened once our sleigh drove away. Matt's words had stung me right to the core. His words, his actions were the reason I'd only ever invented boyfriends in the past five years. I simply wasn't good enough for anyone, in my mind. However, I quickly realized Liam had meant what he'd said.

In fact, as we drove through the tree-covered area that was lit with millions of white twinkling lights, and I'd asked him about it, he confirmed what I knew. Then he kissed me again. We never shared another word on that sleigh ride. We just kissed. Only this time, the kiss was a little different, and it literally took my breath away.

When we returned to the little cafe, we went inside and sat with my parents and my brother. Neither of us mentioned anything that had happened with Matt, nor did we mention anything about kissing one another. When we'd finished our drinks and snacks, we all made our way back to the parking lot and returned to the house. I turned in for the night almost immediately, so I was ready for the full day of shopping today.

I kicked the covers off myself and sat up. I needed to think; I needed a drink, and I needed some comfort food. Opening the door, I listened hard. My parents' bedroom door was closed, as was Joe's. I slipped barefoot out of my bedroom and pulled the door shut quietly behind me.

I made my way downstairs and into the kitchen, where I turned the light on over the stove and put the kettle on. I reached into the cupboard and pulled down a packet of hot chocolate and my favorite mug, followed by the bag of mini marshmallows. It was the only way I knew how to sort through some of my thoughts.

I flipped the switch on the little radio in the kitchen and immediately turned it down. Soft Christmas music played while the kettle finished boiling. I was about to rip open the hot chocolate packet when I felt a large hand on my hip. My body tingled from his touch. I was about to turn around, but I could already feel the heat pouring from his body. I closed my eyes and leaned back against Liam's chest. He gently swept my hair to my other shoulder, his fingers grazing my skin, and kissed my neck.

"I'd hoped it was you up here," he whispered before sucking my earlobe between his lips.

I closed my eyes. My body was on fire as his rough fingers skimmed the soft skin of my hip.

"I couldn't stop thinking about you. From that kiss the first night, then again last night, to tonight. I meant everything I said. If you were mine, I'd make sure that every other man knew it."

Every part of my body was on fire as he kissed my bare shoulder. He placed his one hand on my rib cage, his hand inches from the bottom of my breast. He grabbed my chin with his free hand and tilted my head so his lips could meet mine. Again, this kiss was different, forceful. He was making his claim. I could feel it. It was something no other man had ever done to me.

When we parted, his hands traveled down to my hips, and he pulled me back against him. I could feel him pressing into me. What I felt shocked me; he was huge.

"Do you feel me?" he whispered, his breath tickling my ear.

My cheeks heated at his question. My mouth was so dry I could barely speak, so instead I nodded.

"Do you like what you feel?"

My heart was beating a mile a minute. So fast, in fact, I felt faint. I was sure I'd probably drop on the spot if he let me go. My nipples were hard, my center was throbbing, begging to be touched. I loved what I felt, and it took everything in me, but I turned in his arms and dropped my eyes to the front of his shorts. Biting my bottom lip, I ran the palm of my hand over the enormous bulge. I cupped him in my small hand and loved the sound of the low hiss pass his lips.

"Do it again," he murmured.

Again, I cupped him in my hand, this time watching him as he closed his eyes.

When I let go of him, he grabbed me, placed his hand under my ass, and hoisted me up so I could wrap my legs around his waist. I could feel him between my legs, and my body begged to feel more.

"Want to go downstairs?"

I nodded, wrapped my arms around his neck, and kissed him hard as he carefully carried me down the stairs.

Once in his bedroom, with the door shut, he placed me down on the floor and lifted my shirt off over my head. His eyes dropped to my breasts, then back to my eyes.

"You are beautiful. Every inch of you. Never forget that," he said as he pulled my shorts down. "I also love your ass in these." He ran his hand over my bare ass before lightly slapping it. "Do me a favor?"

"What's that?" I asked, almost breathless.

"From now on, don't wear these around the house when I am with your brother or parents."

I couldn't help but giggle at his request. "Why not?" I asked, trying to be serious.

"Because this is what this does to me," he said, gripping his cock in his hand as he dropped his shorts. "Every time," he whispered, while he stroked himself.

I'd known he was big, but it did not prepare me to see exactly how huge he was. He reached out and took my hand, placing it on himself. Then he pulled me closer, running his thumb over my hardened nipple before giving it a hard pinch.

I'd never been this turned on before, and while I had his cock in my hand, stroking it, he slid his fingers between my legs while his lips meant mine. He slowly guided us over to the edge of the bed. I sat down and brought the tip of his cock to my lips, licking the tip. I loved hearing that sharp intake of breath, and I did it again just so I could hear it one more time before I took him into my mouth.

I felt his hand lace through my hair as I slowly sucked him in and out of my mouth, stopping to lick from the base of his cock all the way to the tip. I was about to take him into my mouth again, but he stopped me, pushing me back and onto the bed.

CHAPTER EIGHT

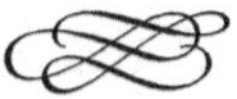

Liam

SHE LAY BACK on the mattress, looking up at me. I knelt down and, starting at her ankles, I began kissing my way up her body, kissing every inch of her until I met her lips. When I slid my fingers between her legs, I felt her jump under me from my touch. When she gripped my wrist, I stopped and met her lips. As she melted into my kiss, I once again began rubbing her.

The instant I slid two fingers deep inside of her, she let out a loud moan. I quickly silenced her with another kiss while my fingers went to work. When I felt her tighten around them, I pulled them from her. Her jaw dropped as I brought both fingers to my lips and licked them both clean.

I reached down into my bedside drawer, feeling around for the box of condoms I was sure I'd put in there. Finally grabbing it, I pulled it out and onto the bed. I tore the lid open to reveal the box was empty.

"Fuck," I growled, more to myself than to her.

When I looked over, a look of disappointment crept over her face.

"Sorry, I sort of fucked this up, didn't I?"

Only the look of disappointment grew into a look of want. A soft smile fell from her lips. She gave me a look of want I'd not seen on her before as she rolled onto all fours before straddling my waist.

"You fucked nothing up," she whispered, bringing her lips to mine. "I'd prefer to feel you with nothing between us."

I adjusted myself and watched as she brought her hands between her legs, gripping my cock. She raised herself up and placed me at her entrance, her cheeks pink as she met my eyes.

"I need to control our first time. You are a little bigger than what I'm used to."

I placed my hand on her hip, my eyes on hers as she slowly lowered herself onto me. "Just take your time," I said, enjoying the tight warmth of her wrapped around my cock.

She let out a small gasp with each inch she took inside of her, and I didn't feel her body relax until she was fully seated on me.

I sat partially up, and gently thrust up into her. She dropped her head back and let out a loud moan.

"Maya, shhhh. You have to be quiet."

She leaned forward and pressed her lips to mine. "Then don't stop kissing me," she said, breathless against my lips.

In one quick motion, I flipped her onto the mattress, my body covering her. I cupped her ass and pumped deeply into her as I kissed her. Her muted moans filled the bedroom, and soon I felt the pressure at the base of my spine. I knew I wasn't far off, and I could tell from how tight she was, she wasn't either. I took my lips from hers, gripped her breast with my left hand, and sucked her nipple into my mouth, as I thrust deep inside of her.

She let out a loud moan as she let herself go over the edge, while I followed.

I climbed back into bed and pulled her against me. Finally, I felt fully satisfied. I'd never had this much desire for a woman, but the second I had been fully inside of her, I wanted to make sure she'd never forget me. I wanted to make sure she knew what it truly felt like to be wanted, to be worshiped, and I'd made sure I'd done just that.

She let out a tiny moan as I pulled her body against mine.

"I should go before everyone wakes up."

"What if I told you I don't want you to go?"

She let out a tiny laugh. "Don't be silly. I have to go. What would my parents think? Better yet, what would my brother think?"

I pulled her tight against me, relishing the feel of how our bodies fit so perfectly together. "I know one way to get you to stay here."

"What's that?"

I slipped my hand between her legs while kissing her neck.

"My parents will be up soon," she said, gripping my wrist.

She pressed a kiss to my lips and slipped out from under the covers, quickly grabbing her shorts and shirt from the floor and slipping them on.

"Just so you know, I'm not afraid of your parents," I said, coming up and wrapping my arms around her waist.

"Neither am I, but we are under their roof."

"This is true."

"I've got to go. I'll see you at breakfast," she said, kissing me one more time before opening the door to my room and quietly heading back upstairs.

MAYA STILL WASN'T DOWN by the time breakfast was over. I'd prolonged my morning coffee as long as I could. Joe came in the front door and looked at me. "Are you ready?"

"Yep, just finished up."

Joe chuckled. "I've never known you to take so long with a cup of coffee. It's like you're making love to it or something."

I choked on my last sip. "Sorry, man. It's been nice to relax."

"Well, we got to get going if you want to see this apartment. The guy said he'd only be there until noon. It's almost eleven."

I placed my mug in the dishwasher and grabbed my jacket and followed Joe out to the car. Minutes later, we were pulling out of the driveway and were on our way to this apartment. We'd just pulled onto the interstate when Joe turned down the radio.

"Can I talk to you about something?"

I nodded, looking out the window. "Sure, anything. What's up?"

"What the hell went on with my sister and you the other night at the festival?"

The second he'd said sister, I inhaled and sucked the gum I was chewing right into the back of my throat that began a violent fit of coughing.

"Jesus, you alright, man?"

I nodded, wiping my teary eyes. "Yeah, just about swallowed my gum. Now what did you ask?" I questioned, my throat still tight.

"I just wanted to know what went on the other night at the festival. I saw the two of you holding hands talking to Matt. She looked upset, but once you came back from the sleigh ride, she seemed different. She was all starry-eyed and just different."

"Oh fuck, he is just a bastard. Do you have any idea what he did to her?"

"I do. I took a round out of him afterward. Maya doesn't know that, but I did."

"Good. However, the things he said, man, I had to protect her. She was a mess. As for the sleigh ride, I just, well, I talked some sense into her."

It wasn't a lie; I had talked some sense into her. I didn't want Joe to think I was taking advantage of Maya.

"Well thanks. I appreciate you looking out for her. However—"

"Look, if you are going to warn me not to hurt your sister, you don't need to."

The car grew quiet. I was almost afraid to respond. When I'd first found out that she was Joe's sister, I'd wished he'd have invoked the bro code. Now if he did, well, I was screwed.

"I'm not deaf. I heard you guys' last night. I will not warn you not to hurt her, because I don't think you would do that. What I want to say is that I want you to be careful because she could hurt you."

"What?" I asked, shocked.

"I know you aren't the type that goes for one-night stands. You were the only one of us when we were on a mission who never partook in those evenings. However, Maya, she is…"

"Tough. I know, she told me. She said it was because of you."

Joe chuckled. "She is tough, but she is also unpredictable. I'm not saying she'd hurt you on purpose, because I know after what she's been through, she'd never."

"Okay. I'm just a little confused."

Joe pulled the keys from the ignition and turned to meet my eyes. "Just be careful. She might seem like she has all her shit together, but honestly, that girl has never taken the time to breathe in five years."

"Man, this is your sister."

"Precisely, and I know her better than she might think."

"Alright, I'll take your warning. Let's go check this place out," I said, shoving the door open and climbing out into the cold winter air.

CHAPTER NINE

Maya

I'D BEEN MORE tired than I thought and woke a little before noon. I'd taken a shower, then made my way downstairs, excited to see Liam. I walked into the kitchen to find my mom working on something for dinner.

"Morning, sleepyhead. I was getting worried. You never sleep this late."

"Well, like you told me before, I must have needed it."

"Well, you were up really late," Mom said, looking my way. I swallowed hard as she studied me. "There is coffee there."

I quickly walked over and poured myself a mug of coffee and sat down at the breakfast bar, grabbing a cold pancake from the plate that sat there.

"How come you were up so late?"

"Couldn't sleep. Had some work things on my mind," I lied.

Just then, my phone rang, and I jumped to grab it from my purse. I looked at my mother, who was still watching me intently. "It's work," I mouthed and made my way over to the couch, praying that by the time I was off this call, Mom would have forgotten what we'd been talking about.

I'd just hung up the phone as both Liam and Joe walked into the house.

"Well, what did they say?" Mom asked, coming into the living room. "I feel you were on the phone forever."

My mom had heard one side of the entire conversation, and I'd known she was chomping to find out what happened. I smiled. "Looks like I got Bali again! They also made me their head travel writer," I said, jumping up and dancing around.

"Maya, that is wonderful. Congratulations on the promotion and on Bali. I know how much you loved it there," she said, standing to hug me. "When do you fly out?"

"End of the week." I looked at my mom and smiled.

"Does being head travel writer mean you will be

traveling more?" Mom questioned, giving me a disappointed look.

As I looked at my mom, I slowly nodded. I'd promised that I'd spend more time at home this coming year and it looked like, with this promotion, that promise had just been broken.

I nodded. "Unfortunately, yes."

I heard Joe mutter something to Liam, and that was when I turned and caught the look on Liam's face. We'd not seen one another since I'd left his room early this morning. During the short time we'd been together, I'd not mentioned much to him about my job, frankly because I didn't think it would matter. I'd not mentioned that my boss may give me the opportunity to travel so soon after the holidays. Although, he'd not asked either.

I'd certainly not meant to sleep with him, yet it had happened. It didn't mean we were in a committed relationship, either. I smiled in his direction only to have him avert his eyes from mine.

"This calls for a celebration," Mom said, heading into the kitchen. "I'm going to make up a charcuterie board, and we'll have wine once your dad is back from the store. Oh, this is so exciting," she said, wrapping her arm around my shoulders and leading me into the kitchen.

We were busy cutting up meat and cheese when Joe came into the kitchen and took a seat at the breakfast bar.

He sat there for a bit watching us both, listening as we talked about my upcoming project.

"Where's Liam?" Mom asked, stacking a bunch of grapes onto the board.

"He went downstairs, said he wasn't feeling very well," Joe replied, looking directly at me, shaking his head, while giving me a glare.

I continued cutting the meat Mom wanted and averted my eyes from my brother.

"So, Bali, huh?"

I nodded. "Yep. It's exciting. I've worked hard."

"And a promotion? That's impressive."

"Thanks," I mumbled. I could tell my brother wasn't happy about my job offer, from the tone of his voice down to his body language.

"Would have been nice had you mentioned it to us. You know, might have been nice not to make us think you'd be around for a while."

I placed the knife down on the cutting board and met my brother's eyes. "Don't do this," I mouthed, looking toward Mom, who had her back turned away from us.

"I, for one, was looking forward to having my little sister around after the holidays. I thought it would give us a chance to hang out and do some winter sports. I know some other people were as well."

"Joe, what is the matter with you?" Mom questioned, turning around, looking at us both. "You should be happy for your sister. She has worked hard. She's getting recognized, and I think it's wonderful."

"Oh, don't confuse this, Mom. I am happy for her. I just wish she'd be careful and consider other people and their feelings. Some people take other's actions at face value. Another thing she should do is stop sending mixed messages. I mean, she gave us no sign that this was coming and yet…here it is."

I looked at my mother and then at Joe. I shook my head. Joe knew. He had to know that Liam and I'd slept together because he sure as hell wasn't talking about him or my parents. They were used to my job by now. I'd seen the look on Liam's face when he heard the news, and now he wasn't feeling well.

"Joe, you will not talk to your sister that way. How was she supposed to know she'd be given a promotion?"

"Mom, stay out of it," Joe said, raising his voice. "This is between me and Maya."

"Don't you dare talk to your mother that way," Dad said, coming into the kitchen. "Now tell me what the hell is going on."

I slammed the knife I'd been using to cut the meat with down on the cutting board. I didn't want them to fight because of me.

"Don't get mad at Joe. This is all my fault." I took off out of the room, rushing past my father. Rounding the corner, I narrowly avoided running into Liam, who'd just come upstairs from the basement. He gripped my arms, but I pulled out of his grasp and ran up the stairs to my bedroom and slammed the door shut behind me.

I flopped down on my bed and listened to the raised voices below me. First, my dad was yelling at Joe, and then I heard Liam raise his voice as well.

I got up, went over to my closet, and began throwing my clothes into my suitcase. I'd fix the fighting. I'd just leave early. I'd shoved everything I'd need for the trip to Bali and then grabbed my other bag that still contained all my travel documents. Then, I put everything just inside the door to my room. Once dinner was over and everyone was in bed, I'd call a cab and head out. I'd leave a note. It was the only way to solve the problem, and I'd gotten used to never staying in one place too long.

CHAPTER TEN

Liam

Dinner had been uncomfortable. Joe wasn't speaking to his parents; Maya wasn't speaking to Joe. She'd said very little to either of her parents, and she refused to make eye contact with me. The table was quiet, and the tension in the room had been unbearable.

Afterward, Joe and I left the house to go out for coffee. He'd explained to me what had happened while I'd gone down to my room. I appreciated the fact that he felt he needed to stand up for me, but I assured him he didn't.

"I just know you. I know you don't get involved with women easily, especially after Candace."

"You are right. I don't."

"I just feel that you'd be perfect for my sister. That's why when I heard you guys, I didn't flip out. It's also why I never invoked the bro code with you. Perhaps I should have invoked the little sister to don't touch my best friend code instead."

We both laughed, then I took a sip of my coffee and sat back. Perhaps I'd made a mistake, perhaps I'd read signals that had never been there. Truthfully, Joe may think I'd be good for his sister, but who ever really knew. Perhaps he'd figured she'd grown up and matured, but maybe he didn't know her at all. Maybe she really was the type not to care. People get jilted all the time from past relationships. Some feel the only way to get back to the one who initially hurt them is to punish all the ones that come into their lives in the present. It works until they realize the only one they are punishing is themselves. I'd seen it with friends of mine. It was also the reason I steered away from having a relationship at all.

"Joe, I thank you for thinking that, and I'm glad you aren't angry at me."

"Nope, I'm not, but I am fucking furious with her."

"Joe, please, let it go. It's fine, really. Don't cause a rift between you and your sister over me."

I didn't want him to feel the need to stand up for me. I knew he cared, but I had a mouth, and I could stand up for myself if I felt it was needed.

When we returned to the house, his parents and sister were already in bed. Joe said good night, but I knew I couldn't sleep. Instead, I went into the kitchen and made some popcorn, grabbed a cola from the fridge, and sat down in the family room to watch a movie. It wasn't what I really wanted to do, but it distracted me from going upstairs and talking to Maya.

I barely focused on the movie, and when it was over, I shut the TV off, bathing the room in darkness. Closing my eyes, I embraced the quietness, focusing on the sound of my breathing. I was just about asleep when I heard the stairs creak. I stilled my breathing and lifted my head to see Maya carrying her bags across the floor to place them at the door.

She stood there looking at her bags, then turned around and jumped, covering her mouth to stifle her scream. "What are you doing there? Trying to give me a heart attack?"

I turned on the small light beside the couch, stood up, taking the bowl of popcorn back into the kitchen. Then I walked over to where she stood, still looking down at her bags.

"I was watching a movie, but it ended and when you came down. I was just laying here in the dark, thinking," I said, brushing the strand of hair that had fallen onto her face. I glanced down at the bags that were placed at her feet. "Where are you going?"

"Don't act like you don't know."

"Well, last I counted, three days haven't passed. So, I don't know," I answered, making my way back over to the couch and sitting down.

She looked at the floor, then walked over and sat down beside me. "Liam, I've messed things up. Everyone is fighting. My brother is angry with me. You are upset, and it's all because of me. So, I'm leaving early."

"Your brother isn't angry at you."

"Then you don't know my brother, because he's certainly not happy with me."

"He's not angry at you. He's upset because he thinks I'm hurt."

She nodded and continued to stare at the floor. "Are you?"

I sat there watching her. She couldn't even look at me. I wasn't sure if I was supposed to take that as a sign that she had feelings or if she really wasn't interested in how I felt. I'd thought I could read her, but I'd been wrong.

"Maya, what is it? Why won't you look at me?"

"It's nothing."

"No, tell me. Please."

We sat there in silence, until she finally looked up at me. "Is my brother right? Are you hurt by me leaving?"

I was quiet. I wasn't sure I was ready to admit

anything. I'd not even admitted it to myself. I didn't normally fall this fast, but there was something about her that from the second I'd seen her, I had to have her. "If you must know, I am. It's probably stupid to think, but I really hoped that something might come of us. I really like you."

She buried her face in her hands. "Don't say that."

"Why not? Is it so hard for you to believe that someone might be interested in you?"

She looked at me with tears in her eyes and shook her head. "I don't know. I thought nothing of it. For once, I just went with the flow of whatever came my way."

I'd been right, I'd read her wrong. I decided this conversation was over and got up off the couch. I should just vanish into the basement and let Maya go about her decision to leave, but when I was halfway across the room, she cleared her throat.

"I also never thought that someone like you would be interested in someone like me."

I stopped and turned around, looking at her. "What is that supposed to mean?"

"Look at you. You're hot and muscular and have a lot of things going for you. While I'm…well I'm this," she said, pointing to her midsection. "I don't have an actual job. Instead, I have a reason to escape from reality."

I made my way back over to the couch and sat back down. I took both her hands with mine and forced her to meet my eyes. "Maya, I like my women soft and curvy. Believe me, I like what I see and what I've experienced with you so far."

I could tell from the look on her face she thought I was giving her some sort of line. I knew exactly what she was thinking.

"Please don't say those things."

I placed my hand under Maya's chin and turned her head, so she was looking at me. "Maya, you are stunning. Easily the sexiest girl I've laid eyes on. However, there is more to you than just that."

"There is?"

"Yes, there is. You are brave and smart. I mean, you travel the world alone. Most women your age wouldn't even think of doing that. You are tough, and you don't get scared easily. I read your blog on Vanuatu. Most people wouldn't even think of travelling again after that. You have this baffling love of pop tarts..." We both laughed. "How the hell can I not be interested in that?"

She let out a tiny laugh. I wanted to lean in and kiss her but studied the look in her eyes instead. It was fear I saw.

"Maya, you need to know that I'm just as nervous as you are. I'm not used to telling anyone how I feel. Like you, I haven't been with anyone in four years."

"Really?"

"Yes." I paused, wondering if I should tell her the

story. It would only open me up to more hurt if she walked away, but then I remembered that I was hoping to establish some sort of trust here. "Remember how angry I got at Matt the night of the festival?"

She nodded.

"Well, like you, I know exactly how it feels to be made to feel as if you aren't good enough and not wanted."

Maya frowned. "What do you mean?"

"Well, you already noticed my demons the first night I was here. When I returned home from the same mission your brother was on, I had a lot of trouble. I had trouble sleeping, coping with small things, and concentrating. It got so bad that I finally sought help. It took a few months, but they diagnosed me with PTSD. I was so happy to know what was affecting me. I went to therapy, and everything was going well, until my girlfriend at the time couldn't grasp what I was dealing with. She came with me to a couple of sessions, but she wasn't open to learning anything. Instead, she pulled away from me. When I needed her the most, she wasn't there for me. She blamed me for our relationship failing, telling me I was weak. What I didn't know was that she'd run into the arms of her best friend, and when I found them together, it was nearly the end of me."

"Oh god, Liam, I am so sorry. You aren't weak."

"I know that now, but my god, it nearly ripped me apart."

She grew quiet and looked down at her hands. She said nothing for a while and then looked up at me. "But why me?"

"Why you?" I sort of chuckled under my breath. She really didn't see what I saw. "From the minute I laid eyes on you in that airport, I think I'd fallen. I felt connected to you. It's something I can't explain. It seemed we were comfortable with one another. It was an amazing feeling. When we left the plane and we parted ways, the only thing I thought about was how I'd wished I'd given you my number. When I realized I'd been too shy to do it, I mentally tore myself apart. Then I met up with your brother, and when I turned around and saw you there, I felt like I was being given a second chance. That night, when I kissed you under the mistletoe, I knew. It was like everything fell into place for me."

"Really?"

"Yes, really," I murmured, leaning in, getting ready to place a kiss on her lips. Instead, I paused when a set of lights flashed through the front window. "Who's here?"

She let out a sigh and turned those sad eyes on me. "Shit, it's my cab. I forgot they were coming."

I tore my eyes from hers. It was pointless. She'd decided a long while ago that she was leaving. Hell, there was a cab sitting in her driveway, and here I was sitting here telling her all this, hoping it would make a difference.

"Well, I guess that's it then." I stood up and shoved my hands deep into my pockets. "Have a safe trip."

A tear slipped down her cheek as she nodded. "I guess it is."

I made my way across the room and stood just outside the basement door. I knew she was standing there staring at me, and as bad as I wanted to turn around, march over to her and pull her into my arms, I couldn't. I heard the closet door open. The silence in the room was beyond deafening.

"Liam?"

I closed my eyes as she muttered my name. I took a deep breath. "You better go before he comes and rings the bell."

I walked over to the basement door, and when I finally gathered the courage to look over my shoulder, I saw the front door close behind her.

CHAPTER ELEVEN

Maya

I climbed into the back of the cab, tears streaming down my face. I was about to tell Liam I wanted to give us a chance, but he wouldn't even turn around and look at me.

"Where to, miss?"

I sniffled and wiped my eyes. "To the airport, please."

I could see the cab driver looking at me in the rear-view mirror. I did my best to hide my face from him, but it did little good.

"Everything alright, miss?"

"Yep," I lied. "Please hurry."

"No problem."

I watched as he set the meter and then backed out of the driveway. I looked up at the front of my home, hoping to see the curtains part, only they didn't. I curled up into the back seat and focused my attention on the passing houses instead of Liam's words.

We finally pulled up to the airport, and the driver helped get my luggage. Once he pulled away, I turned toward the doors. I didn't have a flight booked; I hadn't told my boss I was planning on leaving early. Honestly, I didn't even know what I was doing here.

I walked into the bustling airport and made my way over to the ticket agent to see if it was possible to get a flight. I was soon advised that I had a ticket, but I couldn't change the date. It was a provision my boss put in, and unless I had prior approval, the date he'd chosen would be the one I took.

I walked over and sat down in an empty seat and pulled my phone from my pocket. I began writing an email to my boss, letting him know I was available to leave early, when I heard a woman cry. I turned and looked over my shoulder as I watched her walk through the airport, holding onto a woman's hand. They made their way over to where I was sitting and sat down behind me.

"It's okay, sweetheart. It will be fine," the woman said, doing her best to comfort her.

"It won't, Mom. He's gone," she sobbed.

The lady who was doing the comforting looked over at me. "Miss, I'm sorry, but do you have any tissues?"

I reached into my pocket, feeling the small bundle of tissues I'd shoved in there before I left home and passed her some.

"Thank you," she murmured, turning her attention back to the woman who must be her daughter. "Darling, please."

"No, Mom, you don't understand. I was given the opportunity to work it out with him so many times. Instead, I pretended like I didn't care, and I walked away when I should have done the opposite. Now he is gone forever."

"I know you are hurting," she said, wrapping her arm around her.

"Hurting? Hurting? I'm ruined. He was my everything, and instead, I spit in his face and left. I never told him how I felt, and now it's too late."

Tears welled in my eyes as I sat there listening to this woman cry. I looked down at my phone, reading the email I'd just written as tears flooded my eyes. Was I making a mistake?

"Honey, there was no way anyone could have known this was going to happen."

"You're right, but I'll never know if things could have been different. He was my best friend, and now I'll never know if we could have been something."

"Did you ever think that you weren't ready to hear what he had to say?"

"I heard it all, Mom. He was in love with me, and I so much as shoved it back into his face by walking out. I can't do this. I'm not ready to say goodbye." The woman began uncontrollably sobbing while I sat there reading this email, begging to be sent away early.

I quickly hit reply and began writing another email while listening to this woman cry. I had to do something and knew I had full control over the situation should I choose to give it to myself.

CHAPTER TWELVE

Liam

I FINISHED GETTING DRESSED and made my way upstairs. I was sure everyone was up, judging from the noise going on above my head. I made my way to the kitchen where I found Andy reading

the paper while Marlene cooked breakfast.

"Morning, Liam. Sleep well?" Andy asked as he put the paper down on the table.

"Good, thanks."

"Oh, Liam, I'm making your favorite," Marlene said, pouring me a cup of coffee. "A mushroom quiche."

My stomach let out a growl, and I chuckled. "Thanks. It smells delicious."

"You boys have quite an appetite. I'm not used to all this food." Andy chuckled. "Feel like I've put on ten pounds since you got here."

Just then, Joe appeared, a funny look on his face. He said nothing; he held a letter in his hand and sat down at the table and ran his hand through his hair.

"Want some coffee, sleepyhead?" Marlene asked.

I looked over at Joe as he made eye contact with me. He barely shook his head, but his expression said it all. She must have left a note upstairs before she'd left. He passed the letter to me, and I quickly skimmed it over before passing it on to Andy.

"What's this?" he questioned, taking the letter from me.

"I found it this morning in the bathroom," Joe answered. "It's from Maya. Before you ask, I checked her bedroom. She's gone, and so is her suitcase."

Marlene covered her mouth as she let out a tiny whimper and turned away from us. "Joe, I knew you were being too harsh on her."

"I didn't think she'd actually leave," I muttered.

Andy cleared his throat and looked over at me. "What's happened here?" he questioned me and Joe more than his wife.

Joe sat forward and gave me a sideways glance before looking at his father. I knew there was no way that Joe would tell them about us. But after having talked to her last night, I still felt this was as much my fault as anyone's because I was the last one who had the power to stop her.

"Does this have anything to do with your displeasure about her promotion?" Andy asked, sitting forward.

"How the hell am I supposed to know?" Joe bit out.

Marlene looked at her son. "Joseph, you were horrible to her, and I don't want to hear that you weren't. Andy, does it say where she's gone?"

I glanced at my best friend, silently thanking him for not saying anything to his parents about Maya and me.

"It just says that she decided to follow her path and that we will be better as a family unit without her," Andy said, looking over the letter again. "Dammit, Joseph!" Andy yelled, throwing the letter on the table.

I pulled my phone from my pocket and began checking the outgoing flights to see if there was one to Bali but found nothing.

"We have to look for her," Marlene cried, picking up the letter and reading words that clearly hurt her.

Andy got up and walked with his wife over to the closet, followed by Joe, each of them getting their coats on when I glanced out the front window in time to see a cab pull in. I swallowed hard as anxiety built within me.

"Come now. Let's get going before we are too late," Andy said, reaching for his keys.

He pulled the front door open to reveal Maya

standing on the other side, bags at her feet. Instantly, she burst into tears at the sight of her parents.

Marlene cried as she wrapped her arms around Maya, while Andy brought her bags into the house. Once the door was closed and Maya had slipped out of her coat, Andy hugged his daughter.

"You scared us so much," he said, pulling her to him.

"Dad, I'm so sorry," she cried, hugging him back.

Each one of them hugged her again. No one asked her anything more. They were both just happy to have her back home. When they finally let her go, Maya stepped toward Joe and wrapped her arms around him.

"Look, I'm sorry for the way I acted," he said, while his father stared at him.

"It's okay. I know you didn't really mean those things you said. I love you."

Marlene and Andy stood there, arm in arm, looking happy when the oven timer went off.

"Oh, that is the quiche. Breakfast is ready." Marlene smiled. "Come, everyone, let's devour this quiche."

She and Andy made their way to the kitchen, followed by Joe.

"You guys coming?" he questioned, looking at the pair of us.

"You go. We will be right there," Maya said, nodding to her brother.

Once Joe left the room, I turned my attention to Maya, who stood there watching me. She stepped down into the living room and stopped in front of me, taking my hands in hers.

"I went to the airport with every intention of getting onto a flight and never looking back, until I heard this woman crying."

I frowned and looked at her. "Please tell me you didn't get mugged?"

"I see you read more of my blog."

I nodded. "That small town at the border of Mexico doesn't sound very pleasant, either." I chuckled.

"Well, you will be happy to know that I didn't get mugged. What I heard, though, almost killed me. This woman's sorrow over losing someone she had feelings for before she got to tell him was unbearable to listen to. It got me thinking about the things you said last night."

I kept my eyes trained on hers. She looked at me with fresher eyes than she had only a few hours ago. I swallowed hard as I waited for her to continue.

"You said you were scared. Well, I'm fucking terrified."

I wrapped one arm around her, pulling her closer to me. "What are you terrified of?" I whispered.

She swallowed hard as her eyes became glassy. "I'm terrified of how I feel about you," she whispered.

I cupped her cheek, leaned in, and kissed her. I loved feeling her body relax, her arms moving up around my neck. Once our lips parted, I rested my forehead against hers. "Don't be."

"I also want to tell you I turned my promotion down, and starting Monday, I'm going to look for work here."

"Are you sure?" I questioned, not wanting to get my hopes up to only find myself let down again.

"I am." She raised up her toes to press a kiss to my lips before I pulled her against me.

I held her in my arms, and when I opened my eyes, I saw Joe standing in the doorway to the living room, smiling. Then he turned and made his way back into the kitchen.

"Can I tell you something? When I heard you were leaving, my heart was literally in my throat. The thought of not being able to kiss these sweet lips, or grab that sweet round peach of an ass, almost killed me."

A tear slid down her cheek as her eyes met mine.

"You also need to know that tomorrow when you wake up, after we've parted ways tonight, that I will want you more than ever. It will be torture to sit across from you at breakfast or beside you at dinner and know I have to behave myself."

"Then don't behave yourself," she whispered into my ear.

As she stood there in my arms, I knew that perhaps

we'd started on the wrong foot, and that we'd gone a little too fast. Now, having been given a second chance, I wanted us to take things slow, because I never wanted to lose this woman. Pop Tarts and Mistletoe would forever be my most favorite Christmas memories.

CHAMPAGNE AND FIREWORKS

Champagne and Fireworks

Copyright © 2024 by S.L. Sterling

All rights reserved. Without limiting the rights under copyright reserved about, no part of this publication may be reproduced, stored in, or introduced into a retrieval system, or transmitted in any form or by any means (mechanical, electronic, photocopying, recording, or otherwise) without the prior written permission of both the copyright owner and the above publisher of the book. This is a work of fiction. Any references to historical events, real people, or real places are used fictitiously. Other names, characters, places, and events are products of the author's imagination, and any resemblance to actual events or places or persons, living or dead, is entirely coincidental. Disclaimer: This book contains mature content not suitable for those under the age of 18. It involves strong language and sexual situations. All parties portrayed in sexual situations are consenting adults over the age of 18.

CHAPTER ONE

Everly

I drank back the last of my hot chocolate and dropped my mug into the center console's cup holder. Pushing the door open, I grabbed my bag and climbed out of the car. Snow covered the ground, and as I stepped forward and pressed the keypad to lock the car, I almost slipped.

I looked at the rundown building in front of me. The festive season is a rough time of year for many people, and it always made me happy to help those in need. Many people struggled with financial and family issues, like dealing with the family alcoholic, or they were just plain old depressed, but most people I dealt with were just acutely aware of feeling alone.

I took a deep breath of the icy air and headed toward

the building, thinking of the one woman I'd spoken to last night. She was trying to come to terms with the realization that she'd just broken up with the one she thought was "the one." I hated to admit it, but that one hit home for me, and it was all I could do to fight off the wave of tears I'd felt as I listened to her talk. People's emotions always ran high this time of the year, and I always did my best to keep my chin up, but this year was difficult, even for me. While the holiday hotline filled my nights with something to do, it also gave me a sense of purpose —and I really needed that right now.

I'd spent the better part of the year dealing with my own emotional turmoil. My best friend Maya was a travel writer, and I hadn't realized how much I needed her until I couldn't reach her because of a different time zone. As time passed, I realized that, in some ways, I was glad I hadn't been able to reach her. It was her brother who had broken my heart, so maybe it was better that she wasn't around to listen to me cry over him. In fact, I knew it was better because I cried over him for months. As the holidays approached, I assured myself I'd be okay. I'd made it through Christmas, but then forty minutes ago Maya called me, and suddenly the weight of all that had happened between her brother and me came crashing back down.

I walked into the call centre and hung my coat up in the closet then sat down in an empty seat beside Clara. It was loud in the room as everyone talked about their Christmas.

"I didn't think you were going to show," Clara said, moving her chair closer to mine.

"I'm sorry. I would have been here earlier, but I got a call from Maya."

"Well now, that's a name I haven't heard in a while."

"I know. It shocked me to hear from her as well. She's been travelling a lot for work, and last I'd heard from her, there was a possibility she wouldn't make it home for the holidays because of the storm that they flew into. However, luck was on her side. She was able to get home and is apparently now looking for work locally."

"Local work? That doesn't sound like Maya. What happened to her idea of travel the world, see it all?"

"She finally met someone." I giggled. "And she is over the moon with excitement, and now she wants to fill me in on all the details."

Clara used to hang out with us, until she'd gone off to university. So she knew about Maya's breakup, the one that caused her to decide to become a travel writer in the first place. I couldn't help but laugh when she gave me that knowing look, because the news of Maya looking for local work had been as much of a shock to me as it was to her.

"So, when are you going over to see her?" Clara asked.

"Tonight, after the hotline," I answered, pulling my notebook out of my bag and opening it up to a blank page so I could take down any important notes.

"Everly, I don't want to come across as *that* friend, but are you sure you're ready?" Clara handed me a plate of muffins while taking one for herself.

I leaned forward and reached for a can of soda that was sitting in the middle of the table. Cracking it open, I looked at Clara and shrugged. "It's been a while, and time heals. I am sure I will be okay now."

Clara gave me a worried look. "That voice doesn't sound that of someone who is confident. Is he going to be there?"

I slumped down into my seat. She was right, and deep down inside, I knew it. I'd told Clara everything that happened between Joe and me, but Maya was my best friend, and I would never turn down the chance to see her. Even if it meant I'd run into Joe.

"I know she is your best friend. I consider her one of mine too, but…"

"But what?" I questioned.

Clara shrugged. "I don't know. I just think that she should come to you. I'd never make you come to me if it were my brother who broke your heart. It's only the right thing to do. You shouldn't be forced into seeing Joe again."

"I've kept my issues with her brother to myself. She

obviously knows we broke up, but I always told her I'd be there for her. It's not her fault we didn't work out. So, I'm putting on my big girl pants. I'll be okay." I smiled. "After all, I am trained to handle this sort of stuff."

Clara reached out and placed her hand on my shoulder. "Yes, you are, but someone trained you to deal with these things when it's happening to others. It's very different when they are happening to you."

"Clara, may I speak with you for a moment, please?"

We both stopped talking and looked over at Angela, one of the hotline's supervisors.

"Give me a minute," Clara whispered.

I nodded and sat back in my chair and split my muffin in half while I waited. I listened to the chatter in the room while I thought more about Clara's advice. I'd had a crush on Joe since puberty began. It wasn't a secret. We began dating when we were fifteen and we'd never looked back. Things moved so fast between us that everyone warned us to slow down. In fact, he was the reason I went into psychology.

He'd gone off and joined the military right out of college. Shortly after that, he'd been deployed. So while he went overseas, I stayed here and got my degree. I knew Joe would probably need help once he returned, and I wanted to make sure I was prepared to do just that. Only he wouldn't take my advice and he wouldn't let me help him.

Clara placed her hand on my shoulder. "Sorry about that. Look, I don't want to be a badger, but I guess I'm worried about you."

"I know, and I appreciate it. But seriously, I am good," I murmured, picking up my pencil and doodling on the paper in front of me.

"Everly, why are you are so stubborn? You were upset for months when he broke things off with you. I just don't want you travelling down that road again."

"Yes, I was upset. Of course I was upset. Who wouldn't I be? Pretty much everyone is upset to a degree when they break up with someone, no matter what the reason," I said, shoving a piece of muffin into my mouth.

"All I am saying is that I want you to be careful. You need to be at the top of your game right now. We can't lose you here, especially during this time of year. The hotline needs you, and so do your patients."

I frowned. Was she saying that I'd let her down last year when I took time off after the holidays because Joe and I broke it off? Was she saying I'd do it again because of seeing him?

"What are you saying?" I questioned, feeling defensive.

"I'm just saying I know how you were when you first broke things off. It was like all your training fell completely out of your head. You struggled for a long time, before you said anything to me about the crisis you were in."

"Clara, I thought we were going to get married. Instead, he blindsided me and broke it off over something that wasn't even true. I tried to defend myself, but he wouldn't allow me to. I was beyond hurt. So, of course, I struggled. I also did what I needed to do. I took time off to focus on myself so that I could be the best version of me to my patients. I followed your advice."

Clara nodded. "It was a tough time for sure. I just…"

"You just what?" I asked.

When Clara didn't answer, I turned and met her eyes. I noticed an immediate look of regret in them. I sat back for a moment and looked hard at the situation. She was only expressing her concern for me, and here I was, biting her head off. It was wrong, and I realized it the second I'd looked at her.

"I'm sorry. I shouldn't get mad at you for expressing concern. Perhaps you are right. Maybe the whole situation is bothering me a little. Maybe I'm not ready to see him."

"It's okay, Everly. I shouldn't stick my nose into places it doesn't belong."

"No, you are being what you are supposed to be: a friend, and a good one at that. I mean, when I went off sick, you moved your practice here to work with me. You listened to me moan and groan over him for months. So, I should be the one to apologize."

"Thank you."

Before I could say anything else, a throat cleared, and we both turned our attention to the front of the room. John, our supervisor, stood before us, waiting for everyone's attention. I was thankful at that moment because he was saving me from thinking any more on this conversation.

CHAPTER TWO

Joe

Liam and I parked the car in one of the parking lots near the Christmas festival, grabbed our coats, and climbed out of the car. It was our annual holiday guys' night out and something I'd been looking forward to this year. It was best that I surrounded myself with as many people as possible if I was going to get through this holiday season. I'd hoped that Liam could join in on all the single guy fun when I'd invited him for the holidays; however, he'd quickly quashed that when I found out he and Maya had met and somehow fallen into this baffling insta-love relationship in only a few days.

It had been a tough year for me. I'd started out the new year single, after breaking up with Everly last Christmas, and I'd spent the rest of the year that way too. I'd also been on suspension from work and hadn't been allowed to return until I sought some help for PTSD. The first, combined with the second, was the reason I hadn't been in a rush to run out and get involved in a new relationship. It was better that I'd taken the year to myself, to heal and get over Everly, then once the new year hit, I planned to put myself back on the market. So far, everything was going as planned, except getting over Everly.

"You alright?" Liam asked as we walked to the festival entrance.

"Yeah, why?" I replied, shoving my hands deep into my pockets.

"You know why," he said, giving me a look. "Everly..." he whispered.

I nodded. "I'm okay. I knew we'd see one another again. She is my sister's best friend. I just wasn't expecting it to be now."

"I know that. When Maya announced she was coming by the house tonight, you looked like you were going to be sick. I know it can't be easy having to face her. Especially when it's technically your *holiday*," he said, emphasizing your holiday.

"My holiday?" I questioned.

"Not your holiday... I mean, it's the holiday you two

treasure. Think about it. You initially asked her out over Christmas break. You were going to propose last Christmas, until you broke it off with her instead."

I looked over at Liam, who stood there with a straight face. "You know, you can be a real asshole." I shoved him in the shoulder and chuckled.

"Hey, I'm not the one who broke up with the woman I love because of some stupid rumour. You should have known better, and that was what I told you when you told me what you'd heard. She'd never have turned you in to the department. I think you were just dealing with so much at once, and hearing that just added that inkling of doubt inside of you."

He said nothing that wasn't true. I'd entertained a rumour I'd heard from one guy at work about Everly reporting to my boss about my mental state. It was stupid because I knew deep down it wasn't true. I wasn't her patient, and she had no grounds to do that. Yet one night my boss came to me after I'd panicked and lost my shit during an arrest. They immediately forced me into suspension until I got help with the things I was struggling with. They diagnosed me with post-traumatic stress disorder, just like Everly had said I was suffering from. I'd tried to cope with the situation; I talked to Liam, and then I stopped at a store on my way home from work that morning and found her talking with the guy who'd told me she'd reported me. Anger filled me, and instead of taking a breath, I took it out on us. That was when I broke it off, figuring the rumour had to be true. She'd turned me in.

I heard our names called and turned in time to see Tate, Hudson, and Dax approaching. I quickly turned to Liam. "Please say nothing in front of these guys, okay? I don't want to spend my one night out with the guys thinking about what, or better yet, who, I'll be returning home to. Let's just hang out and have a good time."

Liam nodded. "I can do that, man."

WE HAD dinner and drinks at a little sports bar and then headed back to my parents' place. Mom and Dad had gone to see friends of theirs for the evening, so we planned to kick back in the basement, play some pool, and just be guys. It was rare that we all got a night off together, what with being law enforcement.

"For the game, eight ball in the corner pocket!" Dax yelled out as he bent down and lined up his cue.

"Watch this, ten bucks says he misses just like last time." Hudson chuckled while the rest of us laughed.

"Guys, I'm not going to miss."

"Ha, you say that every time!" Tate replied. "So if

you are so sure you won't miss, how about you put your money where your mouth is?"

"Fine…ten bucks," Dax shrugged.

"Well now, I guess I'll get in on that action," Tate said, whipping out his wallet, pulling out a ten and slamming it onto the edge of the table.

Liam and I looked at one another and then joined in, placing a ten spot each on the table's edge. "Don't mess this up, Dax," I said, tipping my beer bottle back and downing the cold liquid.

We all watched as Dax studied his shot. I swore his hands shook, and he was sweating by the time he actually tapped the ball with his cue. We all watched as the eight ball hit off the bumper and spun away in the opposite direction.

"And of course…. he misses!" Hudson yelled.

The room broke out in laughter, and we all watched as Dax stared at the ball as it rolled into the centre of the table. He then reached around and pulled two twenties from his wallet. "You guys' suck."

"That's okay, you'll have your chance to win this back at the next poker game," Tate said, knowing full well that Dax sucked at cards as well.

"Who's up for another round?" Hudson questioned, shoving his money into his pocket.

Liam looked over at me. "Well, don't look at me. You're the host. Go grab some beers…and bring down the leftover wings, would you?" Liam chuckled. "I'm hungry again."

"Oh, and don't forget the chips I brought," Tate said as he started setting up the table for the next game. "They are in the kitchen."

Rolling my eyes, I made my way upstairs and quietly opened the basement door and poked my head around it, making sure the coast was clear. Maya sat on the couch, alone, watching a Christmas movie.

"She isn't here yet, you coward." She giggled.

I frowned and stepped into the living room, closing the door behind me. "Who's saying I was looking for anyone?"

"Whatever, Joe. She'll be over later."

"Again, I don't know what you even mean by that." I headed toward the kitchen, pulling five beers from the fridge along with the wings. I shoved those into the microwave and bent down to grab a tray from the cupboard. When I stood up, Maya stood on the other side of the island, her arms crossed, looking at me.

"What?" I asked, placing the beer onto the tray first.

"It never ceases to amaze me how easily you lie. I know you came up here to look for Everly. Just say it."

I pulled the wings from the microwave and placed them on the tray, then glared at my sister. "I came up here to get food for the guys, I wasn't looking for anyone," I muttered.

"Right. In case you've forgotten, she volunteers at the holiday hotline during the holidays, so she won't be here until after they close."

"And I said I don't care." I huffed, grabbing the bags of chips that were on the counter and placing them on top of everything else.

"Whatever." Maya leaned against the counter and reached into the bowl to grab a wing.

"They're hot."

She shrugged. "I like hot wings."

"Who's lying now?" I shot back as I grabbed a handful of napkins. I'd just thrown them on the tray when the doorbell rang. Maya looked at me and gave me a smug smile. I knew I needed to get this stuff downstairs before she let her in. I was about to pick up the tray when Maya shook her head.

"Why not wait here? This way she can look her biggest regret in the eyes and you can see how great she is doing without you."

I watched as Maya spun on her heals and made her way over to the door.

"Don't be such a bitch!" I yelled as I picked up the tray and made my way over to the basement door. I'd never shot down those stairs so fast in my life.

CHAPTER THREE

Everly

I stood on the front porch, bottle in hand, shivering. Snow had fallen, and it was colder than I'd expected, and I'd left my hat and gloves in the car. I shoved my keys in my purse just as the door opened. Maya stood there grinning ear to ear and quickly pulled me in for a hug.

"Come in. Come in!" She screeched in excitement as she stepped to the side. "My God, it's so good to see you. It's been so long," she said as I kicked my boots off. "You look fantastic."

"Thanks. It's been too long, but I guess that happens when one of us is a great world traveller." I giggled.

"Stop it." Maya laughed. "I'm not a great world traveller. It's my job."

"No. You are a world traveller, it's true. I've kept up with your adventures on your blog. It looks like you've been staying at some swanky places, lady."

Maya shrugged. "Well, yes and no."

"Yes, and no? Girl, you are crazy. You just spent time in Tahiti. I saw the pictures on your Instagram. That place was to die for! I'm actually envious of your career choice. Look at you all tan and relaxed."

I handed Maya the bottle of liquor I brought and slipped out of my coat, hanging it on the banister just like I used to. "As you can see, I brought the liquor."

"I see that. What did you bring? Goldschlager, Tequila, good ole Moonshine from your dad's basement?" she asked, turning the bottle in her hands until the label appeared. "Caramel Shots?" She made a funny face as she looked at the bottle. "Honestly, I'd have preferred your dad's moonshine. Is there even alcohol in this?"

"Yes, of course there is alcohol in it! And in case you forgot, some of us have to drive home tonight, and Dad stopped making his moonshine years ago."

We both laughed. "You know you can always stay." Maya shrugged, making her way to the kitchen where she pulled two holiday glasses from the cupboard. I watched as she filled them with ice before pouring the creamy liquid.

"I'm sorry, but I'd rather donate my still beating heart to science than sleep across the hall from your brother," I said, sitting down at the breakfast bar.

The room was silent for a moment, until Maya cleared her throat. "Alright then, why don't you tell me how you really feel?" She giggled. "Well, if you are interested in giving up your career in therapy, there is an opening where I used to work," Maya said, shoving a glass over to me. "I mean, you said you were envious of my choice. You can travel and be all tan. Why don't you apply?"

"I figured there would be when you told me you were planning on packing it in. So, why don't you tell me all about him?" I picked up the glass and took a sip of the cool liquid, waiting for her to dish about Liam.

"There isn't much to tell. I met him at the airport on the way back from Tahiti."

I looked at Maya as if she'd lost her mind. She'd met a guy in the airport on her way home for Christmas break and in four days had left behind her job. I cleared my throat and avoided her eyes. She'd be able to tell just from looking at me I didn't approve. "Well, he must be something then for you to give up a job you love."

Maya nodded. "He is. It's like… it was kismet. You

know, like in those silly romance movies we used to watch."

I'd once believed in kismet. Now I just figured it was a pile of crap. "How so?"

"Well, it turns out he was friends with Joe."

I nodded. It was all I could do. Her brother had hurt me so badly, and I feared she was in for the same type of heartache. It probably wasn't right to pigeonhole this guy into the same group as her brother, but like they say… birds of a feather.

"What?" Maya demanded, her glass halfway to her mouth.

"Nothing," I said, feeling tension slide up my back.

"No, I can tell there is something you want to say, so say what's on your mind."

I was quiet for a few moments, taking a sip of my drink, wishing I could come up with something else to ask her. "Do you think that is a healthy choice?"

God, even in my head, I sounded so much like my therapist self that I hated it. I never took the professional work tone with my friends, which proved to me that Clara might have been right. Maybe I wasn't over him, and perhaps coming here wasn't the best idea. I should have had Maya meet me at a coffee shop or something. Maybe in an unfamiliar environment I'd have been more open to the fact that my best friend had found what she thought was the love of her life.

"What is that supposed to mean?" Maya questioned. She reached for a bag of chips on the counter and dumped it into a bowl before shoving it toward me.

I grabbed a chip and shoved it into my mouth. "Sorry. That wasn't called for. I'm sure Liam isn't anything like your brother."

Maya looked at me with concern. "You're still not over him, are you?"

The room grew silent as we looked at one another. I was hoping for a way out of this question and, as if someone was listening, they answered my prayers. The doorbell rang.

I grabbed a handful of chips and shrugged. "Guess you could say I've been saved by the bell." I giggled.

"Don't get too comfortable there. You aren't getting out of this conversation that fast."

I let out a sigh as I watched Maya make her way to the door. I shoved a couple more chips in my mouth and took a deep breath. It was harder than I thought to be back in this house again. The memories flooding my mind were almost impossible to cope with. Joe and I had memories in every room of this house. We'd cuddled and made out on the couch in the living room more times than I'd cared to count. We'd even had a small, brief fling in the kitchen that involved whipped cream and syrup. In fact, it had happened in the exact spot I was sitting.

"It's so great to see you," I heard Bexley say.

"We are dying to hear about this god you've roped," Poppy said.

"Hey, girls." I turned to look at both Bexley and Poppy as they came into the kitchen. "Bet you guys never thought the four of us would be together this time of year again." I giggled.

"That's because you are so busy with the holiday hotline that you've ignored our texts. We've invited you to many things this year, but our invites go unanswered."

I passed the napkins and bowl of chips toward them, while Maya poured two more drinks.

"So, have you seen him yet?" Bexley questioned, sitting down beside me.

"Is he hot?" Poppy asked.

I shook my head. "No, Maya hasn't introduced me to him yet." I shrugged. "There must be something wrong with him." The three of us giggled.

"There isn't anything wrong with him. He's downstairs with Joe, Tate, Hudson, and Dax. If you girls want to go down there, we can."

"Let's do it!" Poppy shouted. "I want to see what this guy has got that the rest haven't."

"Must be an enormous member!" Bexley shouted.

"Oh, my god," Maya mouthed as her face went red.

"That's got to be it, girls. Look at her, she's blushing already," I answered.

I watched as both Poppy and Bexley grabbed their drinks, then grabbed Maya and began marching over toward the basement door. There was no way I was going down there. I grabbed another handful of chips and my drink off the counter and followed the three of them, stopping at the couch.

"Aren't you coming? Surely, you must be curious?" Bexley said, turning around.

I shook my head and sat down. "No, I think I am just going to wait up here for you guys to come back."

"Suit yourself," Poppy replied, pulling the door open.

The girls took off down to the basement, and soon I could hear the commotion downstairs. I closed my eyes the second I heard Joe's voice. That rough, sexy voice I'd always loved. It went hand in hand with his touch. The longer I listened, the warmer the room got, and soon I had no choice but to get up from the couch. I made my way back into the kitchen and began searching their liquor cupboard for a shot of anything to calm this ache inside of me. An ache I shouldn't be having.

I pulled out a bottle of tequila and then went into the cupboard and pulled down two shot glasses, quickly filling them. I had just shoved the bottle back into the cupboard when I heard the basement door open. Taking a deep breath, I glanced into the living room, praying that Joe wasn't with them. Instead, I caught eyes with Maya just as I downed the first shot, which I quickly chased with the second.

"Ummm... I thought you had to drive home?" she questioned as she came into the kitchen and looked at the two shot glasses before me.

"Ha, you were right. We need more liquor," I said, bending and pulling out the bottle of tequila and pouring two more shots. "What was I thinking…caramel shots… I don't know where my head was when I bought that."

Maya stood there, watching me as I poured and downed the next two shots. Once the burn left my throat and I opened my eyes, she looked at me with worry before clearing her throat.

"What?" I questioned, slowly screwing the lid back on the bottle.

Maya gave a little smirk. "Nothing, but I think I'll go upstairs and pull out the sleeping bag."

"That might be a good idea," I said, and then hiccupped.

CHAPTER FOUR

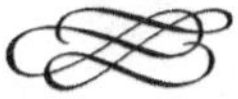

Joe

Poppy and Bexley danced around the pool table after sinking another two balls before missing the third, getting a lead on both Tate and Hudson.

"God, you two are killing it tonight," Hudson said as he studied the table. "Although… I think you're about to go down."

"Don't speak so soon, Hudson," Liam said as he walked by carrying two beers. "Tate will still need a turn, and we know how that always ends."

"Shut up, would you?" Tate said, pointing the pool

cue at him. "Or you can come on over and show me how it's done."

"Gladly," Liam said, chuckling as he leaned over and passed me an open bottle and sat down across from me. "It would be much better than sitting here watching this torture."

We both took a swig of our beer and sat back.

I could hear Maya and Everly laughing upstairs. They'd not come back down here since Maya went upstairs, and I'd yet to lay eyes on Everly. Poppy and Bexley had said they were preparing some food for everyone and would be down once it was ready.

I leaned back in my chair and closed my eyes, listening to the music and Everly's laughter.

"So, tell me, are you going to talk to her?" Liam questioned.

I shrugged. "Not sure I have anything to say really."

"I beg to differ, man."

"Why's that?"

I heard him mumble something under his breath, then he looked at me. "Joe, you know I'm not one to get into things, especially with my friends' relationships. But you are one hell of a miserable dude, and you have been ever since you cut her loose. Now I look at you and I see someone who's depressed as fuck and, to put it bluntly…"

"To put it bluntly? Don't you think you already did that?"

"The two of you have things to talk about. Just say what you feel and get it over with. Move on from this and get back together with her, if that is what you both want."

Just then, the door to the basement opened and Maya appeared carrying two trays full of hot appetizers. Everly followed, carrying a bowl of chips in one hand and a dip in the other. Liam met my eyes and shook his head as I took a swig from my beer bottle. I'd tried to prepare myself and not look her way, but the second she stepped into the room, all I could do was stare.

She was still as beautiful as ever, even if she looked a little tipsy. Her long, wavy brown hair flowed down her back, stopping just above her ass that still looked perfect in the pair of jeans she'd chosen to wear. When she turned around, I immediately noted her light-brown eyes looked a little sad. The happy gleam that they used to have was gone. I let out a deep breath and brought the beer bottle to my lips. Mentally, I was kicking myself for ever believing that stupid rumour.

"Jesus, you look like a little lost puppy." Liam chuckled.

I rolled my eyes and brought the bottle to my lips once again, tipping it back to find out it was empty. I glanced over at Liam, who looked at me with worry.

"Get me another?" I questioned, setting the bottle off to the side.

Liam shook his head. "Sorry, man, I'm not sure that would be wise."

Just then Hudson walked over and passed Liam another beer and was about to hand me one. Only Liam reached out, taking it from him.

"He's cut off." He shrugged, taking the beer and passing it over to Tate.

"What's going on?" Dax questioned, flopping down onto the couch beside Liam.

"Lover boy here is regretting his decision to cut Everly loose last year," Liam replied as if I weren't even in the room.

"Dumbest thing he ever did. Yet we told him that when it happened. Didn't we?" Hudson muttered, smacking Dax in the arm.

"Yep. Damn idiot he is."

"I don't want to talk about this," I muttered, glancing over in time to see Everly glance my way, quickly averting her eyes as mine met hers.

"Why not?" Liam questioned. "It's only the good friends who tell you what an absolute mistake that was."

I blew out a breath and was about to tell them all to take off when Maya wrapped her arms around Liam's neck and placed a kiss on his cheek.

"Hey, gorgeous," he whispered, meeting her lips.

Once again, I looked over at where Everly sat with Bexley. She was looking my way but as soon as we made eye contact, she averted her eyes quickly. I had a feeling it was going to be a long night.

LIAM AND MAYA were curled up on the loveseat in the basement pretending to watch a movie, while I still sat in the same chair I'd been in all night. Poppy had gone home early, as had Dax. I shoved a handful of popcorn into my mouth and took a sip of pop. Tate and Hudson were in a neck-and-neck game of pool with Bexley and Everly.

"It's the last shot. Can she make it?" Bexley giggled, waiting while Everly studied the table.

Everly came around the table and glanced in my direction. She'd been giving me the same look all night, and I'd dated her long enough to know exactly what that look meant. Yet I ran my hand through my hair and looked over toward the TV. When I looked back up, she was bent over the pool table, making my imagination run wild. We'd had a couple of good nights against this pool table, one that I wouldn't mind repeating if ever given the chance and looking at her in this very position brought back very clear memories of that night.

"YES!" Bexley shouted, causing me to jump. "Pay up, fellas," she said, holding her hand out.

"No way. Give us a chance to win our money back!" Tate cried.

"It's getting late. We really should get home," Bexley replied. "Some of us have to work in the morning."

I glanced over at the clock, noticing it was almost two.

"You girls are a bunch of chickens!" Hudson called out.

I glanced over at Maya and Liam and cleared my throat loud enough that my sister looked up at me.

"What?" she muttered, resting her head against Liam's shoulder as he kissed her forehead.

"Aren't you going to walk your friends out?" I questioned rather impatiently.

She looked up at me. "Can't you do it? I'm warm and comfy," she murmured, closing her eyes as Liam kissed her neck. "Besides, it's only Bexley. Everly is sleeping over. I've already put out the mattress."

I let out a sigh. "Fine."

As I followed the four of them up the stairs, all I could think about was the torture I was going to endure tonight knowing that Everly would be tucked into bed across the hall from me.

Once we were upstairs, Everly hugged Bexley. "I'll call you tomorrow," she whispered then waved to Tate and Hudson, who were already getting their shoes on. I glanced over my shoulder to see she had slipped into the bathroom.

"Night, girls. Bexley, did you want a ride?" Hudson questioned.

"I'm good, thanks." She hugged me and then made her way out the front door, with Tate and Hudson following behind.

I said good night to each of them, and then shut the front door and turned to see the bathroom door was still closed. I stood there waiting in the silence, wondering if Everly expected me to walk her upstairs, or if she could put herself to bed.

I walked up into the kitchen and began putting things away, more to quiet my mind than anything else. I'd realized by watching her tonight that the boys were right, I'd made a huge mistake in letting her go. I never should have believed that stupid rumor. I'd just flopped down on the couch when the bathroom door opened and Everly stepped into the living room.

"I think I'm just going to head home," she said, making her way toward the door. She looked down at the floor where her boots lay and let out a sigh.

"Tell you what, if you can get those boots on without

falling over, I'll let you go. Otherwise, I think it's best that you play it safe and stay here tonight."

She gave me an annoyed look and bent over and picked up one of her boots. "See, I got this," she muttered. She lifted one foot off the ground and unsteadily rocked on the other. Before she even got her foot in the boot, she tumbled to the side. I quickly reached out and steadied her before she fell into the wall. She let out a little giggle.

As our eyes met, her smile fell away from her lips, and she nodded. "Thank you. I guess you are right. I'll sleep here."

"That would probably be a good idea," I muttered. "You have fun tonight?" I questioned, following her to the base of the stairs.

She nodded. "It was nice to see everyone."

"Including me?" I questioned.

I moved in behind her and leaned against the railing, getting ready to follow her up the stairs, when she turned around and came face to face with me. Our eyes locked, and my heart beat hard in my chest as I placed my hands on her arms. Fuck, I wanted to kiss her so badly. Just one kiss.

"Joe…"

A shiver ran through me as I heard my name fall from her lips. I wanted to hear it again. I missed it so much; I hadn't realized it until this very moment.

"What?" I whispered, leaning in so close I could feel the heat from her body.

Her eyes met mine, and for a moment, I was almost sure she was going to meet me, but she placed her hand on my chest to maintain what little space we had between us.. I was almost sure I could see tears in her eyes.

"I need one Joe-free Christmas this year," she mumbled, looking at me with sad eyes.

My heart sank. I didn't really know why I expected her to say something different. I'd broken her heart.

"So, I'm going to say good night. Good luck in the new year, Joe." She leaned in and placed a light kiss on my cheek, turned and made her way upstairs to Maya's room.

CHAPTER FIVE

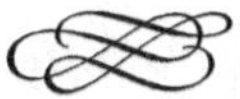

Everly

"I call it the New Year, New Me Plan," I said, shoving the piece of paper I held in front of Clara. I'd been doodling on for the past two days while at home.

I watched as she picked up the piece of paper and read it while she sipped her coffee. I'd been proud of myself for coming up with such an extensive plan after spending the other night in tears at Maya's.

"Well, it's a start," she said, reading the list I'd come up with on how to get myself back together. I watched her expression as she continued reading. Concern flooded me when her brow furrowed and she glanced up at me.

"How did the other night go?"

I shook my head. "I'm not really sure I want to talk about it."

"I see," Clara said, looking at the sheet of paper before placing it on her desk. "I think you do."

I frowned. "You do? How on earth would you know what I'd want?"

Clara chuckled. "Well, judging from your list, he's all you want to talk about."

"Huh?"

"My dear, do you realize his name is in every single point listed on that piece of paper? So, unless Joe is your new name…"

"No, it isn't," I said, getting my back up.

"Look for yourself." Clara chuckled, shoving the list my way. "You have put his name with every single point you listed."

I glanced down at the list in front of me. She was right. Every point I'd written contained his name. I had littered it all over the page. My heart sank as I stared down at it.

"Give yourself a break," Clara said, looking at me with concern.

I ripped the page off the table and crumpled it up in a little ball while meeting her eyes. "So much for that," I muttered. "I've got to get back to my desk. Talk to you later."

"You know we can always sit down and go over some things if you like. I'm open to helping you."

I waved over my shoulder and shook my head as I grabbed my mug of coffee and left the office. "No need. I'll just be miserable forever."

I heard Clara giggle as I walked away, knowing full well that wasn't the truth, but at the moment it seemed like it.

When I returned to my desk, I set my mug down and threw the crumpled piece of paper into the recycling bin under my desk and sat down. I flipped on the small overhead light and turned on my monitor then switched my phone on to receive calls to my desk. I jumped when it began ringing almost immediately.

"Hello, this is the Holiday Hotline. Everly speaking, how can I assist you tonight?"

"Oh thank god, I found you. I've been calling and calling."

"Poppy?" I questioned.

"Yes. I'm so glad I found you. I was getting extremely worried."

I frowned. "Poppy, this is the hotlines' number. I can't tie up the line on a personal call. You should have called me on my cell."

"Well, I tried that. I also tried calling your home

number for the last couple days. If you'd answer it, or listen to your messages, you'd see I have tried. So, I tried to reach you where I knew you'd be—or should be. Where you've been hiding?"

I let out a sigh and took a sip of my coffee. "Sorry, I guess I've been busy."

"You guess you've been busy?" Poppy said, her voice going into that high-pitched screech I hated. "You've been busy avoiding us, and I get it. I really do. However, New Year's Eve is around the corner, and Maya and Liam want to have us all over for the night."

I ran my hand through my hair and sat back in my chair, grateful to be volunteering that night. "Sorry, no can do. I have to be here until midnight."

"You better be kidding."

"I'm not."

"Bexley told me if you don't come she is going to murder you, just an FYI." Poppy giggled.

"Then perhaps you should call the murder prevention hotline. You know, save a life."

"Everly, I'm serious. You need to be there."

"I'm serious too. Listen, I've got to go. I'll call you later."

"I mean it Everly. Do not hang up this phone. We need you there."

"I'll call you later," I said, ending the call and hitting the incoming line that was flashing. "Hello, Holiday

Hotline, Everly speaking. How can I assist you tonight?"

"Finally! Thank god!" Bexley muttered into the phone. "I thought for a moment you'd gone AWOL."

"Not you too!" I said, bringing my forehead to the cold surface of my desk. "I'm going to tell you the same thing I told Poppy. I can't tie up the hotline's number, and I'm volunteering New Year's Eve. Call me later," I said, quickly ending the call before she could start on me as well. The second the call ended, I hit the button for the incoming line.

I half listened to the voice on the other end of the line. I tried hard to focus on what the person was saying, while the voices in my own head got louder and louder. Before I knew it, the only thing I could think of was the other night, standing at the base of the stairs with the man who'd broken my heart, yet still held so much of it.

Two hours later, I packed up my bag and carried my mug to the small kitchen. I washed it and placed it upside down in the dish tray to let it dry and made my way back to my desk. I shut the small light off and hit the power to the monitor then grabbed my bag.

"Everly, before you go. May I speak with you?"

I turned around to see John in the doorway to his office, holding a folder. I smiled. "Sure, John." I took a seat across from him and placed my bag at my feet.

"Everly, I really want to thank you for such

outstanding volunteer work this year. You've certainly made a difference around here for the Holiday Hotline."

I smiled. "Well, what can I say. Helping is in my blood."

"I know. That is why I hope you'll come on board next year."

I frowned. "Of course I will. You know that."

"I never assume. Things change in peoples lives, and I never want anyone to feel as if I don't respect their boundaries. Now, unfortunately, you have hit your maximum volunteer hours this year, and you know we cannot allow you to go over those. So, until next year."

"Wait, what? I am supposed to help on New Year's Eve and New Year's Day. I'm on the schedule," I said, pulling my phone from my bag and opening my calendar where I'd placed my hours.

"Yes, but like I said, we can't have you go over on those. The board members won't like it, nor will your workplace or the governing body. So, that was why I wanted to see you before you left tonight, to thank you for your outstanding volunteer work. You've gone above and beyond as always. We are lucky to have you here," John said, holding out his hand for me to shake.

Shocked, I slowly stood up and took his hand in mine. It wasn't every day that you got dismissed for going over your volunteer hours, or maybe one did. I had put in a lot of extra nights this year, which had probably eaten up those hours that had been allocated for New Year's.

I smiled, feeling filled with dread. "I guess I will see you next year."

"Wonderful, look forward to having you back."

I was just about to my car when I felt my phone vibrate in my pocket. Without looking at who it was, I quickly answered.

"Oh amazing. She answers!" Poppy exclaimed.

Instantly, I remembered our conversation from earlier, and now I realized I had no excuse why I could not go to Maya's on New Year's Eve. The hotline had been my reason, and now that had literally backfired on me.

"Yes, Poppy. I answer my phone."

"Whatever you say. Now about New Year's. I am the one responsible for letting Maya know… So, is it safe to say I can put you on the list?"

"Poppy…"

"Everly, it means a lot to Maya that you are there. So…"

I didn't feel like fighting with her. It had been a long day, and I'd dealt with many tough people tonight. I could always just say I was working at the hotline, regardless, and hole up in my apartment. No one would ever know, I thought to myself.

"Don't think of coming up with an excuse," Poppy

added. "I will remind you; I do drive by the hotline on my way to Maya's, and I know the number and your extension."

I'd forgotten. I swallowed hard and let out a defeated sigh. "Fine, put me down, and now I am going to go home, have a hot bath and a glass of wine. Night, Poppy."

"Night, sweets! We will see you tomorrow night!"

CHAPTER SIX

Joe

"Coffee?" Dax questioned as he pulled the patrol car into the parking lot of the corner store.

"Yeah, I could use one," I replied.

"Be back in a second," Dax said, hopping out and heading into the store.

I leaned back against the seat and sighed. Tonight was our last night shift, and this would be the first New Year's Eve we would have off in three years, and we were both looking forward to it. I was about to close my eyes when a movement caught my attention.

I watched as a figure walked across the dark parking

lot, finally stepping into the light. It was Everly. I frowned. Why the hell was she by herself? This wasn't the best neighbourhood. We patrolled it far too often.

I kept a close eye on her and watched as she stepped up beside her car and fiddled with her purse to get her keys. I was so focused on her, I didn't notice Dax had climbed back into the car and was now sitting beside me, waiting for me to take my coffee.

"For someone who wanted this, he sure as hell is slow grabbing it," Dax grumbled.

"Geez, I'm sorry," I muttered, taking the coffee cup from his hand.

"What the hell are you looking at?" Dax asked, setting his cup in the cupholder and securing his seatbelt.

"Isn't that Everly?" I nodded in her direction.

Dax looked around, finally spotting her at her car. "Yep, it appears so. The Holiday Call Centre she volunteers at is in this plaza, just behind the store, actually. They must have just gotten out tonight."

I couldn't take my eyes off her. I didn't like the fact that she was alone in the dark. "They should light this lot better," I grumbled.

"Did you want to go talk to her?" Dax questioned.

"No, no, not at all. I just want to make sure she is safe."

"Hmm, I see. Well, there is nothing stopping me," he said, grinning ear to ear as he put the patrol car into reverse and backed out of the parking spot, speeding over to her car. He quickly stopped, put the car in park, and rolled down his window.

"Everly! It is you!" he yelled.

She jumped, her spine straightening. "Dax?" she said, looking over at the car and squinting.

"Yep, just me and good ole Joe here. We thought we'd come over and make sure you were okay."

"Hey, Everly," I called.

Her entire demeanour changed the instant she heard my voice. Her face and shoulders held a ton of tension, and instead of answering either of us, she quickly shoved her stuff into the back seat of her car and waved.

"Good night."

Dax let out a whistle, rolled up the window, and looked over at me. "Wow, she really hates you, man. You are right."

"I know," I muttered.

Dax waited until she'd started her car and pulled away before exiting the parking lot and pulling onto the street heading toward the downtown area. "So, New Year's Eve party this year. Sounds exciting."

"Cool. Where is that at?" I questioned, finally taking a drink of my coffee.

"Did you not get the invite?" Dax questioned, pulling over to the side of the road.

"Can't say I did."

"It's at your parents' place."

I frowned and looked over at Dax. "Do my parents know?" I chuckled.

"Of course. They are heading out for the night to a party of their own for once. It's going to be like old times, man," Dax replied, then cleared his throat. "Well, practically exactly like old times."

"How do you figure?" I questioned.

Dax let out a laugh. "Parties when your parents are out are amazing and, like a few of those old times, before you got together with her, you, my friend, will sit in the corner and stare longingly at Everly."

"How the hell would you know? You weren't even there when that shit happened."

"Maya told me."

I cleared my throat, irritated by this entire conversation. " Since when did you start talking with my sister?" I asked, feeling on the defensive for absolutely no reason.

"Since you broke your brain cells and broke up with Everly last Christmas. We actually talk a lot."

I chuckled under my breath. "And I guess that would make that your longest relationship then? The one with my sister?"

Dax met my eyes. "We're just friends. She is your sister, after all."

I looked out the window at the park we parked beside. "Didn't stop Liam, now, did it?"

"I'm going to ignore that comment. Not going to drag poor Liam into this, but in his defence, he had no clue she was your sister when he met her. Also, unlike Liam, I look at Maya as a little sister. Now, I guess you'll be at the party?"

I sat there for a few moments, thinking about the other night with Everly standing at the base of the stairs. Her sad eyes, her perfect lips at the forefront of my mind. I'd have given anything to feel her lips against mine again, to hold her in my arms again. I should have just taken charge of the situation and kissed her how I used to. It would have only been a matter of minutes before she melted in my arms and…

"Earth to Joe."

"What?"

"So, are you going to be at your own party?"

"Is Everly going to be there?" I questioned, once again allowing my thoughts to travel back to the other night.

Dax shrugged. "I don't know. I guess you'll have to be there to find out."

"You're an ass. You know that."

Dax chuckled as he placed his coffee in the cupholder and began pulling away from the curb so we could continue our patrol.

I QUIETLY SHUT my bedroom door and stripped out of my uniform. I laid my pants and shirt on the back of my chair and reached for my boxers that lay on the bottom of the bed. After turning the TV on, I made my way over to my dresser, pulling open the top drawer. I shuffled things around, finally finding what I was looking for.

I pulled the little black box out and held it in my hand for a moment, running my fingers over the soft velvet. I closed my eyes, standing there thinking for a moment, and then lifted the lid to stare down at the 1-carot round, brilliant-cut diamond set in white gold. As I looked down at the ring, it was then that things hit me. How horrible I'd been to her. Her face flashed before me, her eyes full of tears that wet her red cheeks as they fell down her face.

I closed my eyes as I heard the words I shouted at her after the department had notified me of my suspension. It had crazed me with anger, and I was looking for anyone to blame but myself. The rumours had been floating around that my girlfriend, the psychologist, had been the one to rat on me for having difficulty and that was why I was being suspended. It had nothing to do with my actions during the arrest. While I'd heard the rumours that my enemy was spreading, I'd known better. The news of my suspension had somehow made it true in my mind that she had turned her back on me.

That morning, she'd just gotten out of bed and was sitting waiting for me like she always did, curled up on our couch in her boy shorts and tank top, when I came in through the door like a hurricane and fucked our relationship up for good.

If I'd had my head on straight and had gotten the help I'd known I needed when I'd returned from my tour, then none of this would have happened. We'd be engaged and deep in the planning stages of our wedding. Instead, a few weeks later, I gave notice to my landlord and moved back home with my parents, and in order to keep my job, was forced to start therapy.

I shook the thoughts from my head and squeezed the tiny box closed. I flipped it open again and stared down at the ring. She'd never gotten to even see the ring I'd bought her, and I'd never taken it back, because somewhere deep inside of me, I hadn't been ready to give her up. After seeing her the other night, I realized she was to be with me. Now I just needed to figure out how to get her back.

CHAPTER SEVEN

Everly

I let out a deep breath as I pulled up in front of Maya's and cut the engine. Joe's car sat in the driveway. I'd hoped he would have plans for tonight and that he wouldn't be here, but I'd been wrong. I reached for my cell phone to see where the hell the girls were. Neither Bexley nor Poppy's car were in the driveway, and it looked as if Maya wasn't either. Which probably meant Joe was the only one here, and there was no way I was going into the house alone.

I quickly typed out a message and hit send and sat there waiting for a response. I leaned back against the seat and closed my eyes, letting out a yawn. I was more tired than I thought. I hadn't realized it until this morning when I could barely get out of bed. I had been working too many hours between the hotline and my own practice. As I sat here, I was thankful that my practice didn't open until the sixth.

I glanced at my phone to see if either of them had responded, but there was nothing, then I glanced up at the house. I'd made it an entire year without him. That alone was something to celebrate, and there was no way in hell I was going to backslide now. I'd almost done it the other night. I'd almost fallen into his perfectly bowed lips.

I grabbed my phone and quickly typed out another message to my friends and went to put my phone back down when the tap on my window caused me to jump. I let out a loud groan when I saw Dax standing there, smiling.

I rolled my window down. "Dax! Jesus, you scared the shit out of me."

He chuckled. "Well, miss. We've had many complaints about a stalker out in front of this house. You wouldn't know anything about this, would you?"

I smiled more to myself than to Dax. Leave it to him to lighten the mood. "I was just leaving, officer."

"Hmmm, I don't know about that. The car isn't

running, my dear. I think we are going to have to take you inside."

I could see the humour in his eyes. "Are you…are you going to throw the book at me, sir?"

Dax chuckled. "No, I think having you and Joe in the same room will do the trick. One of you will sing like a canary in no time." He chuckled again, opening the door to the car.

"It will be him. I have nothing to confess," I said, climbing out of the car and hugging Dax hello. I went to grab my bag, but he stopped me and grabbed it, throwing it over his shoulder.

"I hope you know that I have to listen to him talk about you every day. It's painful as hell."

I met his eyes and nodded. "I hope you know I don't think of him at all," I said, looking away as the lie fell from my mouth.

Dax wrapped his arm around me and leaned into me. "If that were true, you wouldn't be here tonight looking like you were going to be sick." He kissed me on the cheek before letting me go as he waited for me to climb the stairs to the front door.

"Maybe I'm just a great friend, Dax. Maya means a lot to me."

Dax shrugged as he pressed the doorbell. "That may be, but I really think it's more than that."

MAYA HAD SHOWN up along with Poppy, Bexley, and Liam almost as soon as we were inside, and I hadn't ever felt more relieved. While Poppy and Bexley followed Joe, Hudson, Dax, Tate, and Liam to the basement, I went upstairs with Maya to put my things in her room. She'd made me swear that I'd spend the night and have a good time tonight.

"Now, I'm hoping that Mom and Dad aren't home early, but if they are, after they are in bed, I'm sneaking down to be with Liam, so you can just sleep in my bed."

I nodded while I pulled out my pajamas and placed them on the end of her bed, not saying anything but beginning to feel uncomfortable at the fact she wouldn't be here with me tonight.

"Are you okay?" Maya questioned, looking over her shoulder at me as she put a few things into a bag.

"Yep," I murmured.

I could feel her looking at me, studying me, and I knew she knew I was lying. "Everly?"

"It's nothing. Let's go," I said, zipping up my bag and latching onto her arm, pulling her toward the door.

We made our way down the stairs and were just in

time to say good night to Maya's parents before we made our way to the basement. Laughter erupted from the basement as we came down the stairs, and all eyes turned to me. Maya grabbed a cooler from the mini fridge behind the bar while I stayed over near the stairs.

"No way. Get over here," Poppy said, coming over and grabbing my arm, pulling me over to the bar where Joe stood mixing drinks for everyone. "You are not playing hide in the corner. Now, what do you want?" she asked.

Memories flashed through my mind of one of the last times Joe played bartender, and I feared if I wasn't careful, tonight may end up the same way it had then.

"Rum and Coke, Blue Lagoon, Dirty Martini, Sex on the Beach…" she said, pulling at my arm as Joe looked my way.

"I'll pass," I mumbled.

"No way will you pass!" Bexley screamed.

I couldn't help but laugh at her reaction, or at the fact that Poppy was shaking me so hard she was spilling her drink all over the floor.

"Fine…fine…I'll have a gin and tonic." I laughed just as Bexley grabbed hold of me and began shaking me as well.

"Gin and Tonic it is," Joe said, grabbing my favourite gin and quickly mixing the drink. He slid it in front of me and then brought over a slice of lime and placed it in my glass, giving me a wink.

I softly smiled, knowing everyone in the room had their eyes glued to us, and took my first sip.

MAYA AND LIAM danced with Bexley and Hudson in the centre of the room. Joe and Dax sat over in the corner talking, while I sat on the barstool watching Poppy and Tate in a game of pool that was now neck and neck.

"Are you ever going to talk to the poor soul?" Bexley asked, taking a break for a minute from dancing. She sat down next to me and grabbed a bottle of water, taking a swig, before returning to her vodka cooler.

I wanted nothing more than to talk to him. The want grew stronger with each drink I'd had and with each look he'd given me. However, I would not be the one to cave. If he wanted me, then he'd have to work to get me back. I shook my head. "He hurt me, Bex. If he wants me, he's going to have to work for it."

"I know he did."

"He also needs to learn never to do it again," I muttered.

"Bex, get over here," Hudson called.

"Have another drink," she said, getting up and returning to Hudson, Maya, and Liam.

I couldn't help but laugh while I watched them dancing around like crazy. I drank down the last of my gin and tonic and set my glass on the bar behind me as Dax looked over at me as he walked to the washroom.

"Want another?" I heard Joe's deep voice ask.

I glanced over my shoulder at him and nodded.

He began by pouring the shot of gin in my glass and then looked at me. "Are you ever going to talk to me?" he questioned.

"I never said I wasn't talking to you," I replied.

"Then can we talk?" he questioned, topping my glass up with tonic and adding a fresh slice of lime.

"If we do, will you leave me alone?"

The intense look he gave me sent shivers through me, just like always. He was so sexy, and I wanted to take back those last words. I didn't mean them. "If the talk goes well, I don't plan on ever leaving you alone again."

"Don't hold your breath," I muttered, even though I didn't mean it.

Joe walked around to the front of the bar and took hold of my hand. "Come with me."

I slowly got up off my stool and looked at everyone else, but no one was paying any attention to us, or at least they were pretending not to be. I followed him to the spare bedroom in the basement, which was now Liam's.

"If you think you're going to get me in that bed, think again. You aren't that charming," I said as Joe shut the door behind us.

"I'm not trying to get you into bed. We aren't having sex…yet, that is." He grabbed my hand as he sat down on the edge of the bed and pulled me down beside him.

"No, we are never having sex again. EVER," I gritted.

Joe chuckled at my response. "Everly, I made a huge mistake letting you go. I want us to have another chance."

I swallowed hard; I wasn't sure I was ready to hear this. I wasn't sure I was ready to accept his apology, and I feared he really wasn't ready to give it.

"Another chance? After everything that happened?"

"Yes, had I of gotten the help I needed when I returned from the military, like you asked me to, none of this would have happened in the first place."

"I get that, but it happened, and even though I told you I didn't do what you were accusing me of, you didn't believe me. So, what is going to happen the next time someone tells you some stupid rumour? Are you going to go all ape shit on me or are you going to give me the benefit of the doubt?"

"I was wrong to do that."

"Yes, you were. You weren't even considering me, you wouldn't listen to me. I'd never been so hurt in my entire life. We'd been together for years. Never once had I broken your trust, and as if I were some girl you'd only known a couple of months, you simply took someone else's word over mine."

"I know. I said it was wrong. I wasn't using a logical thought pattern. I was angry, and I allowed that anger to overtake the situation."

"Yeah, but even after a couple of weeks, I called and tried to talk things through with you, and you refused to hear me out. You were more closed off then ever. I fucking tried to stay, to give you the space I knew you needed, but you wanted nothing to do with me. Your words, if I remember them correctly, 'Anyone who stabs me in the back will always be my enemy, you included. I don't want to see your lying face again,'" I repeated, raising my voice.

"Everly, I was angry. I was lost. I've spent hours and hours in therapy, and I've worked on myself. I've also worked through us. After I came back, I had no clue why you wanted to be with me. I was broken. It made little sense to me that this woman I loved, the woman of my dreams, wanted me."

I got up and began pacing the room. I didn't know what to say to him. I knew he'd had problems when he returned. I knew he needed to work through them, and I wasn't a stranger to even telling my patients that some-times couples needed time apart to realize what they had with one another. In fact, I'd just given that advice out to a couple I'd been counselling for months.

"Everly…" Joe whispered.

I didn't respond. I just kept pacing back and forth, gin and tonic in my hand, while looking at the floor.

"Everly…did you hear me?"

"I'm trying to sort through all of this, Joe. I just can't forget everything and say okay, it's fine. It's done. I don't work that way."

"Well, if I can get you to kiss me by midnight, will you see me again?"

"You better be kidding," I spat and stopped pacing and looked at Joe. The look in his eyes was sincere. He meant it. I swallowed hard, debating how to answer him.

"Everly…please."

"How do I know you won't do this again?"

As I stood there, he got up off the edge of the bed and walked over to me. He slowly took the glass from my hand and placed it on the dresser, then he pulled me into his arms. My body flooded with heat as he pulled me against him and looked into my eyes.

"Give me a chance and let me show you how I feel," He whispered as he ran his fingers through my hair before placing his hand on my cheek.

My entire body flooded with emotion as his lips

grazed mine, slowly at first, and then with more force. My body betrayed me while my brain tried to deal with my emotions that it didn't know how to break down and unpack. As we stood there kissing, anger flooded my system, and I pushed him away.

"Everly, what is it? I thought…"

His words were but a whisper as tears burned behind my eyes.

"I can't do this. I just…" I tore open the bedroom door and flew out of the room, past our group of friends and up the stairs. I could hear Maya, Bexley, and Poppy calling my name, only I didn't stop. Instead, I flew right up the stairs to Maya's room and slammed the door shut behind me.

I was struggling. There was no doubt about it. The feel of him near my body, his lips on mine, had done me in. A huge part of me wanted nothing more than to be back in his arms for good, but a much larger part of me was afraid of getting hurt again.

CHAPTER EIGHT

Joe

I stepped out of the bedroom and noticed all eyes were on me. Bexley stood beside Maya, both with their arms crossed, as did Poppy. Liam, Hudson, Tate, and Dax all looked over at me as well, not with quite the same look as the girls, but still they all stared.

"What the hell did you do?" Maya yelled, taking a step forward.

Liam went to grab her arm, but she shrugged out of his grip and took another step toward me.

"I did nothing," I replied.

"Well, Everly's reaction seems to tell a different story," Bexley added.

"Yeah, she went upstairs in tears," Poppy replied. "That can only mean one thing. You did something."

"Why does it mean he had to be the one to do something?" Dax demanded from where he sat in the corner.

"Oh please, don't tell me you think she did something," Bexley questioned, turning to look at Dax.

"You woman need to calm down," Hudson said, stepping up beside Bexley and trying to turn her around from giving Dax the death glare.

"Don't touch me," she gritted, pulling out of Hudson's grasp.

"Joe, whatever you did, you best undo it. Don't mess up this holiday for her, too," Maya spat, taking another step forward, making me feel like she was going to attack me.

"Whoa, slow down there, sweetie. No need to get all up in his face," Liam said in a calm voice, placing his arm around her waist. Only instead of listening to him, she turned and gave him a look that I thought would knock him to the ground.

"You know, I think everyone just needs to calm down for a minute." Tate groaned, placing his cue down on the pool table. "Why don't you girls head upstairs and see how Everly is doing? Us men will have a talk."

I looked at my sister, disappointment filling her face

as she looked at me and shook her head. Liam took her hand and pulled her back into his chest, placing a kiss on the side of her neck.

"Go on. I'll deal with him," he whispered.

He'll deal with me? What the hell was that supposed to mean? Whatever it meant satisfied Maya, and with one more death glare, Poppy, Bexley, and Maya all headed upstairs, leaving the five of us alone.

I'd never felt more of a weight off my shoulders than I did once those girls were gone. The guys were far less judgmental. We all headed toward the couch and chairs, while Liam grabbed five beers from the mini fridge and handed them out. We each cracked our beer open and took a drink.

"Fuck, those women are ruthless," I said, tipping the bottle back, drinking down the cool liquid.

"That they are! Now why don't you tell us what happened in there?" Dax questioned, tipping his bottle back again.

"Leave out nothing either," Liam answered, grabbing a chair and straddling it.

"Tell us all the juicy bits, too." Tate chuckled.

I scraped at the label on the beer bottle and looked up at my friends. "Look, all I did was apologize. We talked about what happened, then I bet her I'd kiss her before midnight and she'd have to return to me."

Liam shook his head and ran his hand over his face,

while both Tate and Hudson groaned and did the same thing. Dax looked me directly in the eyes and shook his head.

"Did you actually kiss her in there?"

"Fucking right I did."

Dax said nothing. The other guys all let out another groan and took another drink.

"You actually just marched right up and planted one on her, knowing full well she was having a hard time with everything that happened between the two of you?" he questioned.

I nodded.

"God, Joe. I can tell you right now, that was a mistake, my friend," Dax replied. "I've heard it all from your side, and I've heard it from her side. You can't just go in there and try to get some. She isn't that type of girl. She needs to feel safe, respected, and that she can trust you."

"She knows all those things," I said, getting my back up.

"Does she? Did you give her the opportunity to actually defend herself? If you had, that would have shown respect. Did you not fly off the handle at her, smashing your fists into walls? Maybe had you not of done that, she would feel safe with you."

"Fuck you, Dax!" I shouted.

"Whoa…" Liam said, standing between the two of

us. "You head outside with Hudson," he growled to Dax while Hudson got up and nodded toward the door.

Once they were gone out the door, Liam sat back down.

"Wow, I really fucked up, didn't I."

The nods were enough from the two of them. I sucked back my beer, and then I heard the sliding door open, and I glanced over to see Dax and Hudson come back into the room and sat down with the rest of us. The room grew quiet as tension filled the air.

I looked over at my friends, all of them avoiding eye contact with me, except for Dax; his eyes were glued to me.

Liam cleared his throat while looking at Dax. "Joe, you needed to talk to her. Not demand things from her. You needed to work her up, to get her to warm up to you. The hurt she's been dealing with isn't surface hurt. It's deep inside. Seriously, man, you will not undo all that hurt with a fucking kiss and some macho attitude."

"You know better than that, Joe," Hudson joined in. "You need to work through this with her, the same as therapy."

"Dax, Tate, what do you guys think?"

"Giving her some stupid line about if I kiss you before midnight, go back out with me…she isn't a piece of meat. She has feelings, man," Tate replied, while Dax nodded.

"Then what the hell do I do?"

"Well, first, no matter how desperate you are to get laid, slow that the fuck down," Hudson said quietly.

"I'm not." I shrugged.

Tate chuckled. "We are guys. We know what it's like to go awhile without. And you, my friend, have gone a long-ass while—"

Hudson smacked Tate across the back of the head. "Not helping."

"What? It's true," Tate said, rubbing the back of his head.

Liam sat up straight and cleared his throat. "You need to just take your time with her. Work through the things that were the problems and take it slow. Let her take the lead, because I can guarantee you weren't listening to a thing she said in there. You were lazer focused on getting her back."

"She needs to feel heard. She needs to feel safe with you again. She needs to know that you will not hurt her again. That all takes time," Dax replied.

Just then Maya, Bexley, and Poppy stepped into the rec room and looked at us. They all went over to the bar and quickly got themselves a drink and came over to where we were sitting, none of them saying anything.

"Is she alright?" I questioned.

Bexley and Poppy nodded. "She'll be fine."

Liam reached over and turned up the radio, while

Tate and Poppy went back to their game of pool. Bexley, Maya, Hudson, and Liam all started dancing again, leaving Dax and me sitting there looking at one another.

"So, what are you going to do?' Dax questioned.

I shrugged. "I guess I'll just back off for a bit. Let her come to me."

"Good plan," he gritted.

I was behind the bar making more drinks for everyone, while Hudson and Dax went upstairs to get some finger foods to ring in the New Year. Everly still hadn't come downstairs, and as badly as I wanted her to be here with me, she needed to decide to join us. I wasn't going to beg her. I was going to let her come to me, and we'd work through things when she was ready.

Hudson and Dax came down carrying two trays of pizza, chicken wings, and some chips, and placed them on the far end of the bar. Everyone came over, grabbing some food and their drinks. As they huddled together, I began cleaning up the mess I'd just made when I saw a shadow coming down the stairs and Everly crept into the room.

She met my eyes and shyly smiled as she came over

to the bar. I was about to offer her a drink when she asked for one instead. I quickly made her gin and tonic and passed it to her, topping it with a lime after the fact and winking at her.

The others still hadn't noticed she'd come down, and when I went to wipe off the bar, she leaned over to me. "Can we talk?" she whispered, her breath tickling my ear.

Instead of announcing to everyone that Everly was here, I went around the opposite end of the bar and made my way to her, taking her hand gently in mine. I didn't pull her down the hall to the bedroom. Instead, I allowed her to take the lead. She led me up the stairs to the quiet of the living room and over to the couch where we both sat down. I waited while she took another sip of her drink, and then she placed that down on the table in front of her.

"Joe…I'm…I'm sorry about earlier. I'm confused. I didn't know how to handle all of that. I…oh boy, how do I say this," she muttered under her breath.

I looked over at her to see she was biting the nail on her thumb, deep in thought. "You just say it," I replied quietly.

She looked over at me and nodded. "You do not know how much I've missed you."

Her words shocked me. I had no idea she even still cared about me, to be honest. Even though she'd been giving me those brief glances the other night, I just thought she hated me. "What?"

"I still love you. I…I missed you. When you came back from deployment, I knew that there would be issues. I was right, it messed you up. It didn't take a trained individual to know it. Anyone could have seen it."

I nodded. "I know. I was out of control over many things. Not just in our homelife but work as well."

"You were. You blamed me for a lot of things, Joe. Many things. Then the night you got suspended, all those things you said the morning that you came home drove such a wedge in between us that there was no undoing it. No matter how bad I wanted to stay and work things out with you, there was no way to do it. You ended us. Afterward, as time passed, I knew it was for the best, for my sanity, but for my safety."

I nodded. There was no way I could deny anything she was saying. I was awful to her, and the guys were right, violent as well. They'd been the ones to help me patch the holes I'd punched into the walls because I was angry. They'd seen it.

"I want you to know that I have gotten help. I spent months in therapy talking things over. I've worked on my anger issues. I thought I was strong enough to work through those things on my own. I know I'm not. Which is why I am still seeking counselling. I still see the therapist that work made me see."

"Is she helping you?"

I nodded. "Very much."

"That's what matters."

She sat there looking down at her hands in her lap. She never used to be one who wouldn't make eye contact. I guess that is what I got for treating her like shit. Being around me had broken her, or perhaps I had broken her. I didn't know which it was.

"We've talked about us in therapy," I said, reaching out and taking her hand in mine.

She finally glanced up at me and waited for me to continue.

"I've talked about wanting you back."

"I see."

"I realize after speaking with you downstairs, I can't just say I've changed and expect that you will believe me. You need to actually see the change first."

"It would help. I mean, I'd love to just take your word for it and just be back in your arms, but I'm afraid. I'm afraid of those things happening again, and I know for a fact that it would break me more than I already am."

"That would not be my intention. I didn't intend to hurt you last time, and I know saying that I was having issues isn't the right thing. I've accepted what I have done. It was wrong. So, I am asking you for your forgiveness."

"I know you didn't intend to hurt me. I too have sought help, Joe. You can't take all the blame for everything. I made mistakes too. I went about things the wrong way, thinking I knew how to handle what you were going through. It's so much easier when it's happening to patients than when it's happening in your own life." A single tear ran down her cheek as she met my gaze. "So, I forgive you," she said as she slipped her hand into mine and leaned over to press a kiss to my cheek. "I hope you'll forgive me as well."

"For what?" I asked, taking her hand in mine.

"For not coming around sooner."

As she slowly pulled away, I took my chances and placed my hand on her cheek and brought my lips to hers. She didn't pull away. Instead, she kissed me back, slowly at first, then she wrapped her arms around me and pulled me in.

CHAPTER NINE

Everly

I wanted that kiss to last forever. The second our lips connected, it felt as if everything was right with my soul. My body didn't seem so lost, and I seemed to be comforted by his touch. Honestly, the few minutes that we shared that kiss seemed to be the most relaxing and warm moments of my entire year.

"We should probably head on down to the basement where everyone is. That way they won't come looking for us. I don't want to give Maya any reason to come up here and find us like this."

I couldn't help but giggle. Joe had always been afraid

of Maya, and I didn't blame him. She could be ruthless if she wanted to be.

"I don't see any reason to hide. We were only kissing." I giggled.

"Well, you weren't downstairs only a few short moments ago when she was ready to remove my male appendage. If it hadn't of been for Liam, I'd probably be bleeding to death on the carpet."

"Everly."

"Here she comes. I told you," Joe said, looking over his shoulder as if he were afraid of what might come his way.

"Everly," Maya called again, her voice getting closer, the sound of her footsteps on the stairs.

"Please answer her."

"We are on our way downstairs!" I yelled out as Joe's eyes pleaded with me.

I leaned over and kissed him before we both got up off the couch and made our way downstairs where we joined our friends.

THE KISS JOE had delivered earlier that night was the only thing on my mind. As our lips parted, we cheered with the rest of our friends. Soon after, we said good night to them, and then I headed up to Maya's room. I'd been laying here for a good hour. I'd heard Maya's parents come home and go to bed. I'd also heard Joe come up and go to bed as well, and it was killing me knowing he was only a few steps away from me, across the hall.

I rolled over and tried to get comfortable, and then tossed again. Maya was downstairs with Liam. There'd be no way she'd know if I snuck across the hall to be with her brother. However, it would break a promise to me. The promise to make sure he was being truthful with me.

I kicked the covers off and got up. Quietly, I opened the bedroom door and made my way to the bathroom, where I once again brushed my teeth. Once finished, I opened the bathroom door, shut the light off, and stepped out into the dark hallway to see Joe standing outside his bedroom door. He wore a pair of low-hung boxers, the band sitting right below the deeply carved vee all women love. My eyes travelled down to that spot and back up to his face. He'd been working out; he'd never been that cut before.

"Having trouble sleeping?" he questioned.

I nodded, biting my bottom lip. "Yes," I squeaked out.

He took a step toward me as his eyes ran down my T-shirt-clad body. Once he was near, I could feel the heat pouring from him, and a shock ran through me as his hands connected with my sides through my thin material.

"Why don't you—"

I didn't wait. Before I even knew what was happening, my lips were on his, my tongue washing through his mouth. He held me tight and backed up to his bedroom door, shoving it open. He pulled me against him, spun me around, and shut the door behind us. Holding me tight, he pulled my mouth against his, kissing me hard as he backed us up to the edge of his bed.

"Fuck, I've missed this so much. I've missed you," he whispered as he pulled my shirt over my head.

His one hand held me, while his lips kissed mine. His other hand cupped my breast, his thumb running over my nipple. I could feel a strong pulsing between my legs, so strong it felt as if I could explode at any second. I could already feel his hardened cock through his boxers, and I allowed my hand to run down and cup him. The instant my hand was on his cock, he let out a low guttural moan that went straight to my centre. I was about to rub him when I felt his hand travel down to my belly and slide into the band of my panties. The anticipation was almost too much, but his fingers quickly found their way and slid through my slit, causing me to moan out loud.

He pressed his lips harder to mine as his fingers danced over me.

"Shhhhh," he whispered, backing me up a little more until my knees hit the edge of his mattress. I sat down and looked up at him. He bent down and kissed me, pushing me back until I was lying on the bed. He looked down at me, that look of pure desire, pure want, radiating from him.

His rough fingers gripped the waist of my panties and he locked eyes with me as he pulled them from my body. He dropped them to the floor and then placed a hand on each of my knees, shoving them open.

"I'm going to take you, Everly. Take you so long, so hard, that you are going to forget your name. You are going to forget everything that happened between us. This is what this night is about. You and me, starting over together. Starting over, this time forever."

He dropped to his knees, gripped my waist with his large hands, and placed a trail of kisses from my knee to where my legs met my body. He repeated the same on the other side. My centre was aching with want, and I wanted nothing but his tongue there. He didn't give me what I wanted. Instead, he licked my bare pussy, one side and then the other, but not the centre.

"God, Joe..." I cried. "Please give me what I want."

"I want nothing more than to taste this sweet pussy, but I'm not giving in to myself—not yet. I've tortured myself this long, not having you," he mumbled as he sunk his teeth gently into my inner thigh. His hands gripped my waist tighter as he did the same on the other side. I knew he was probably leaving marks, and for once, I didn't care. I wanted to be marked by him. I wanted to remember in the morning.

I lifted my head off the mattress and looked down just as he sunk his tongue in between my legs, licking me from the bottom to the top, where he concentrated on that little bundle of nerves. I wanted to scream, but instead I bit my bottom lip and ran my fingers through his hair as I watched him. I could already feel my orgasm building as his tongue worked relentlessly.

"Joe..." I moaned.

He didn't stop. Instead, he moved forward with more force, more everything as he licked and sucked me even harder. I let out a small cry as he slid two fingers inside of me, curling them until he hit that special spot deep inside of me. Instantly, I felt myself let go, and I dropped back on the bed, breathing hard with my eyes closed. I felt the bed dip down, felt his hand slide underneath me as he pulled me against him. He kissed the side of my neck, his fingers dancing over my skin.

"I think I forgot how that felt," I muttered, my eyes closed as I tried to catch my breath.

"I can guarantee you forgot what that felt like."

He grabbed hold of me and, in a swift motion, rolled

back over with me on top of him. "You know what else I think you've forgotten?" he questioned.

I looked down at him and shook my head. "What's that?"

I felt him reach between us and line himself up at my entrance. "How does this feel?" he said, as he held me in place while he slid himself up into me. I sunk down on his cock, taking every inch of him deep inside of me.

"You are right," I murmured as a shiver passed through me and I closed my eyes. He felt so good buried deep inside of me. I didn't want this night to end. He gripped my hips with his hands and guided me, moving me in slow guided moves.

I could hear his breathing getting more ragged with each pump he delivered. I leaned myself forward, my hands resting on the headboard as he licked and sucked at my nipples while he continued working himself inside of me. He held me tight as we both tried hard to hold onto our climax.

He quickly rolled us over, so I was now on the bottom, and wrapped me in his arms, kissing me hard as he slowed down. This was where I wanted to be forever, in the safety of this man's arms. I'd missed him, my body had missed him, and I knew there was no going back now. We needed to work on things, yes, and I knew that if we gave each other the space and the chance we needed, we'd be back to normal before we knew it.

CHAPTER TEN

Everly

Six Weeks Later

I stood looking out the window, over the park while waiting for Joe to get ready for tonight. Since we'd gotten back together on New Year's, we'd both worked hard to bring our relationship back to where it had been prior to all the shit that had happened. Tonight we were cele-brating moving in together and six weeks of the new us.

"You ready?" he asked.

I looked up and caught his reflection in the window. I softly smiled and turned to see him dressed in dark jeans and a black button-down shirt. He'd already rolled the sleeves up to show off his muscular forearms.

"I am," I answered.

"You look beautiful, by the way," he whispered as I stepped past him, his hand automatically moving to my lower back, guiding me.

"Thank you. You don't look too bad yourself. Where are we headed?"

"It's a surprise." He winked, pulling the door open and guiding me out into the hall.

We drove for a bit, and finally Joe pulled into the parking lot at the water's edge. I frowned and then looked over at him. "What are we doing here?"

"You'll see." He winked, shutting the engine off and opening his door.

"What are you up to?" I giggled.

He wrapped his arm around me and led me into the park along the water's edge path. Then we turned down another path and continued on. The excitement was killing me, but Joe was tight-lipped. He held my hand, a small smile on his face, but said nothing.

"Joe, come on. Where are we..."

The words stopped as in front of us I caught sight of Bexley, Maya, and Poppy standing at the edge of a picnic table, making sure it was set perfectly. Above, in the trees, strings of white twinkle lights shone above, and I couldn't help but smile.

"Come on..." Joe said, gently tugging on my arm.

"What is going—"

I stopped again as I saw Hudson and Dax cooking on a small barbecue across the way.

"Oh, they are here," Bexley announced as she caught sight of us. "Is dinner almost ready?" she growled at Hudson.

"Just about."

"Oh, finally, here is the wine," Maya said, taking the bottle from Liam and placing it on the table.

Joe tugged gently on my arm again and moved us forward as I stared in confusion at what was in front of us.

"Welcome, sir. We have your table right over here," Maya said, waving her hand over to the covered table.

Joe led me over and waited while I sat down. As he slid into the other side, Bexley worked on opening the bottle of wine and pouring some into our glasses.

"I believe this is your favorite wine, miss. Meiomi Pinot Noir." She winked as she poured some into Joe's glass.

I smiled, still in shock. Once she'd poured the wine, the three girls went over to where the boys stood, leaving us alone.

"Joe, what is all this?" I questioned.

"This, my love, is a little surprise." He winked, picking up his glass. "To us."

We clinked our glasses together and drank.

"Alright, for the lady we have a filet, medium well, and for you, sir, we have a filet medium rare. We also have one rock lobster tail each and a double baked potato," Hudson said, quickly plating everything before placing it in front of us.

"Oh, and don't forget the sides of mushroom and onions," Dax said, bringing over the bowl and placing it in the centre of the table. "Made it myself." He smiled at Joe, causing me to laugh.

"Enjoy."

With that, the five of them began to disappear, but not before the soft music began playing.

"This looks wonderful." I smiled.

Once we'd eaten, Joe came around and held out his hand. I slid from the table and we began to dance right there in the park under the lights. I rested my head on his chest as we swayed to the music.

"Have you enjoyed your evening?" he quietly asked as his hands rested on my hips.

"So much," I replied, placing a kiss on his lips.

Suddenly, he stopped moving and kissed me once again. When he pulled away, he met my eyes. "Everly..."

I gave him my full attention. I could tell from the serious look on his face whatever he was about to say was important.

He reached into his breast pocket and dropped down to one knee.

"What are you..."

He held his hand out. A beautiful solitaire diamond on a white gold band sat between his fingers. "Everly, we've been through so much. I don't want to experience life without you by my side. I did it for a year and it was the most horrifying thing I've experienced. Would you—"

"Yes." He didn't need to ask anything else. I wiped the tears that had already fallen from my eyes and nodded.

He slid the ring onto my finger and then stood up, wrapping me in his arms and lifting me off the ground as he spun me around before kissing me. Behind us I heard our friends applauding and whistling. As he kissed me again, I heard the champagne cork pop, and Bexley, Poppy, and Maya all whistled. We turned back to our friends, who had the Champagne poured for everyone, and a wonderful looking chocolate cake sat in the centre of the table.

We'd both started out the year away from one another; it was the break we'd needed to see if our relationship was strong enough to bring us back together. We'd both worked hard at realizing our mistakes and working through any issues that may still remain. We'd probably work at this forever, and that was okay because I'd realized that he was my everything, and there was nothing more important than making things work with him.

SUMMER NIGHTS AND FIREFLIES

Summer Nights and Fireflies

Copyright © 2024 by S.L. Sterling

CHAPTER ONE

Hudson - January

"How's the man?" I questioned, dropping the bag of pop onto the table beside the box of pizza I'd ordered. "Does he satisfy you in every way imaginable?"

I turned around to see Bexley staring at me, her cheeks displaying a hint of pink, her eyes disappointment.

"He isn't doing the job is he?"

I'd run into Bexley last week at a coffee shop in town and was shocked that she was there on a date with a guy we knew nothing about. She'd threatened me to keep it a secret, which I had done.

"Oh my god, what do you think I am?" Bexley questioned, crossing her arms.

She didn't need to continue; I'd known she'd been sleeping with him. It wasn't just from her body language when she'd introduced me, it was the reminder not to tell anyone as I took my order and went to leave.

"I think you are a healthy woman with a sexual appetite. Nothing wrong with that. However, I also think you are wasting that appetite on someone who isn't doing the full job."

God I loved how easy it was to get under her skin. I couldn't help but chuckle; it was too easy.

She walked over to me and looked me directly in the eye. So close to me, in fact, her breasts were just about to touch my chest.

"Hudson, what are you saying? Is there someone you think could do better?"

I swallowed hard as I stared into her eyes. She brought her hand to my shoulder and ran it down my arm.

"Well? If there is, you best tell me."

It was as if someone had sucked the oxygen from the room. I tore my eyes from hers and stepped back. It was when I caught the glimpse of a smile on her lips I knew I'd backed down at the wrong time. Bexley was always testing me. She always had. It was what I loved about her. It was also what had gotten me thinking about asking her out. Until I found out she'd met mister right.

"Come on, grab the plates," I said, changing the subject completely.

"What's wrong? Did I hit a nerve?" she whispered, her lips practically grazing the shell of my ear.

I closed my eyes, took a second to regain myself, and then looked at her. "No, you didn't hit a nerve. I was just concerned. Sex is sort of like pizza. You can get it from an excellent place, or you can get it from somewhere mediocre. How would you feel if I got this pizza from Vic's?"

She looked at me and squinted her eyes. "Did you get this from Vic's, because I told you I wanted great pizza."

I chuckled. "See what I mean, and no it didn't come from Vic's. It came from our usual place."

She closed her eyes as her face relaxed. "Thank god," she muttered to the ceiling.

"Do you make that face after sex with the god?"

I flexed just in time for her to punch me in the gut with her fist. I couldn't help but chuckle as she shook her hand.

This was our relationship and I loved it. There was only one thing I'd change about it, but I'd been too afraid to take that step because I knew I wasn't ready for it.

CHAPTER TWO

Bexley - September

"Okay, girls, here's your breakfast."

I gave our usual server what I referred to as my get-by smile—the one I used when I was forced into a situation I didn't want to be in, like this one—as she placed our orders in front of each of us.

It was our monthly girls' Sunday brunch date, the first one I'd been to in a few months. The first one ever since the accident. I'd seen my friends, of course, just more one-on-one instead of a group environment.

"So, does anyone have plans to attend the summer festival?" Maya questioned as soon as everyone had their food in front of them.

"I won't be here. I'm heading up to my parents' cottage for an end-of-summer vacation."

Poppy went to her parents' cottage every summer. She'd never missed it, so it didn't surprise me she was leaving.

"What about you?" Poppy asked Maya.

"Liam and I are renting a bed-and-breakfast on the outskirts of town for a week. We figured we could use a little time away from my 'rents." She winked.

Liam was still staying with Maya's parents. He had planned on getting an apartment with Joe, Maya's brother, until Everly stepped back into the picture and they moved in together. He'd just started on the force a little after Christmas and was still saving for a place.

"Are they getting to you or are you having a harder time sneaking around?" Poppy questioned.

Maya let out a laugh. "Well, obviously they know we are together. However, they don't want us 'doing it' under their roof," Maya said, using air quotes. "My dad was very specific with that."

Poppy and Everly both let out a laugh. "Little do they know you two have been sneaking around since the beginning. When is he planning to get his own place?"

"He said he was going to look again soon. There has been little available that is affordable in the last couple of months. Of course, my parents are thrilled to have him staying with us."

"Of course they are. You can't get pregnant if you aren't 'doing it'." Everly said, using air quotes again and winking.

Everyone at the table laughed, while I poured some hot sauce on my eggs and took a bite of my bacon.

"What are you doing, Bexley?" Maya questioned.

"About?"

"The summer festival?"

I shrugged, taking a bite of my lightly buttered toast. "I don't think I'm going to go." I sighed.

"Why not?"

Once again, I shrugged. "I don't know, don't feel up to it. Plus, none of you guys will be there."

Maya looked over to Everly. "Aren't you and Joe going?"

Everly shook her head. "No, Joe has something to do for work that night, some special project that he can't talk about, and I have to run the support line that night at the office. It was supposed to be Clara's turn, but she is away at a conference."

Maya shrugged, giving Everly a look that she probably thought I hadn't seen, but I had. She'd been doing this every time I'd been around, which had been little. I mean, you hit and kill someone with your car and see how often you want to leave the house.

"Please stop doing that," I mumbled.

"What?" Maya questioned, shoving a forkful of food into her mouth.

"Stop acting as if I can't see your expressions. You are sitting right in front of me," I barked.

The girls all stopped eating and looked at me. I'd been a little less tolerant of things that never bothered me before. The expressions being one of them. I'd changed in so many ways in the past few months, and I knew it worried my friends.

"I think Maya is just worried about you, as we all are," Everly said, taking her therapist tone.

She'd been doing that a lot too when I was around. That ever-so-calm voice hoping to not have me blow up at something one of them said. Every single one of them looked at me differently.

"I'm fine." I huffed.

"How did that date go?" Poppy asked, trying to change the subject.

I thought back to what she was talking about and shook my head. Maya had suggested I try using one of those dating apps after the accident. She'd bugged me about it so much, I finally allowed her to build me a profile and help me pick some guys. I'd known it was going to be a mistake.

I let out a sigh. "It was a nightmare. Won't be doing something like that again."

"Yeah, those dating apps can be messy," Poppy replied. "I had one date from hell off one."

"Thanks for that warning," I muttered. "Regardless, I'm not really all that into dating right now anyway."

"You know, I've been thinking about you putting yourself out there on those dating apps, and it doesn't sit well with me. What if you were to meet someone through friends?" Everly questioned.

I looked up at her as if she were crazy. "Through friends? I don't think so."

"Yes," Maya interjected. "Why didn't I think of that?"

I could feel her wheels at work already. I sighed again. "Well, since I hang out with all of you every night, and we have a small circle of guys that join us, who would be the ones introducing me?"

"Duh, me, of course." Maya shrugged, beating Everly to it.

I shook my head. "I'm good, really."

"Oh come on. I was actually talking with Liam the other night, and we have someone who might just be perfect for you."

I shook my head. "I doubt it. I know everyone you know."

"Are you seriously telling me no right now?" Maya said, sitting forward, Everly and Poppy joining her.

"I am. I'm not interested."

"How can you say that? You don't even know who it is."

Everly leaned in and whispered something to Maya, then she whispered back, and then they both turned and stared at me. Alarm bells were going off inside of me.

"Alright, well, tell me this, is he actually blind?"

Maya glanced at both Everly and Poppy before looking back to me. "No, why?"

"Well, I was thinking, if he was, then I could wear yoga pants, put my hair in a messy bun, with no makeup, and then and only then might I agree to go." I shrugged.

"Hate to break it to you, but no, he isn't blind. Just do this for me."

I picked up my coffee and took a sip. Then shoved a piece of mango in my mouth, shaking my head. "Why? I already told you I'm fine, and I did the online dating thing for you. I don't think I need to do more."

"Well, I'm worried about you. We all are. We are all worried that you might just give up and be alone and miserable for the rest of your life."

It was true. I'd thought about giving up. The accident, the aftermath, had been hell for me. It wasn't just the accident, either. It was the fact that the guy I'd been seeing and hiding from my friends had broken it off with me shortly after that accident because I wasn't fun to be around anymore.

"How about this?" I made eye contact with each of them. "How about, I'll think about it?"

Maya clapped her hands together and began lightly bouncing on her chair with excitement. "Sounds good to me."

To Maya, that automatically meant I'd said yes, which I hadn't. I cleared my throat, placed my hand on her arm, catching her attention, and looked her directly in the eyes. "I said I'd think about it."

I opened the door to my one-bedroom apartment and stepped inside, flipping the light on in the kitchen. I placed the bags that contained the few things I'd picked up from the store on the table, along with the bag of books I'd purchased. I grabbed my sweater off the back of the chair and quickly unpacked the bags and put the food away, before grabbing a can of soda from the fridge. I picked up the books and carried them into the living room. Leaving one on the table, I shoved the rest on my bookshelf and sat down.

The apartment was quiet, almost too quiet. I'd never noticed it before today. Flipping the TV on for background noise, I picked up the book I'd chosen and opened it up, reading the first page. I struggled to concentrate and finally shut the book and put it back on the table.

This had been happening too much. My mind wouldn't shut off. I dropped my head back and stared up at the ceiling. Maybe I was totally unhappy here, I thought to myself. I wasn't one to think of myself as miserable. I used to be the one to laugh, to cause others to laugh and to have fun with my friends, but as I looked back on this morning's brunch, I realized I was only going through the motions.

Each laugh was forced, and I realized I'd only agreed to go to get Maya to stop asking me and because it was something we always did. I hadn't said yes because I'd wanted to go; I was perfectly happy staying at home and alone.

I was literally going through the motions. I wasn't living.

I let out a sigh and picked up my phone. I opened up my chat between Maya and I and started a new message.

Bexley: Got a minute?

Maya: Hold on...

Bexley: Okay

. . .

I SAT STARING at my phone, then saw the little dots bounce. I smiled to myself, thinking of Maya in the restaurant this morning, all giddy because I'd told her I'd think about her blind date suggestion.

Maya: What's up?

Bexley: I have a question for you.

Maya: Okay

Bexley: This blind date…

Maya: Hold the presses. You want to go?

Bexley: I didn't say that. I want to know who he is.

Maya: That, my dear, I refuse to tell.

Bexley: Then no.

Maya: Come on, you can't say no because I won't tell you who it is.

Bexley: Yes I can.

Maya: If I tell you, you'll say no, anyway. Plus, it might ruin it if I told you.

Bexley: You are impossible.

Maya: Yes, so I've been told. Does that mean you will go?

I TAPPED the edge of my phone, contemplating who it could be, but no one came to mind. Dax was, well, Dax. Tate wasn't my type, and Hudson, well, he was just a loner.

Bexley: Fine. I'll go.

Maya: :) YAY!!!!!

Bexley: When is it?

Maya: I'll have to get back to you with those details. Leave it with me.

Bexley: Maya???

Maya: Leave it with me.

Bexley: What have I done...

I GIGGLED to myself as I typed those last words. I set my phone beside me and took a sip of my soda when my phone vibrated. I picked it up.

Maya: You just agreed to what could be the best thing to ever happen to you. Talk soon ;)

CHAPTER THREE

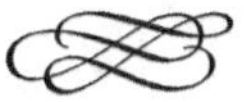

Hudson

"Come on, Dax, sink the damn ball this time," I grumbled, taking a drink of my beer.

Joe and Liam chuckled as we all watched Dax do his best to miss the damn shot again, causing us to once again lose the game against Liam and Joe.

"Sweet bloody victory, again!" Joe sang, giving Liam a high five.

I shook my head as I racked the balls again for the next game.

"Sorry, Hudson, thought I had it this time," Dax groveled.

"Of course you did. Next time, I want a new partner." I chuckled.

Pool with the boys. It was a typical Sunday. I took comfort in doing the things that were routine. Spending Sundays with the boys was routine, and I'd already decided I'd never trade it for the world. It was just the location that had changed. Instead of Joe's parents' place, we stood inside Joe and Everly's new place. It had been a challenge to get the pool table in, but with a lot of persistence, a lot of muscle, and Bexley's brains, we'd made me.

"I'm gonna grab some beer. Anyone want?" Dax asked, heading to the kitchen.

"Anyone want...what do you think?" I said, smacking him across the head as he walked by.

"Do you believe that guy?" I grumbled. "Makes me lose money and then actually has to ask if I want another beer." I chuckled.

"You'd think he'd have gotten the hang of the game by now. It's only been what, eight years?" Joe said, causing us all to laugh.

"What you guys laughing at?" Dax asked, coming into the room with four beers.

"Nothing," Liam answered, passing him his cue. "Get ready."

I was just about to break the balls when the door to the condo slammed shut and I heard a familiar voice call out to Liam. I stood up and turned to see Maya come into the room. Saying nothing to anyone, she made her way across the room and into Liam's arms. Once their lips attached, I figured it was game over, but the next thing I knew, she was staring at me with a shit-eating grin.

"What?" I questioned, worried about what she was going to ask. "Go back to making out with Liam and leave me be." I chuckled, as did Dax and Joe.

"No, I need to talk to you."

"To me?" I questioned. "Why me?"

"Thank god, finally someone other than me is in trouble," Joe muttered, sitting down on the couch and putting his feet up on the coffee table.

"And me," Liam added.

Maya turned and looked at him, smiled, then placed a kiss on his lips. "You are never in trouble, baby."

Joe stuck his finger into his mouth and faked a gag.

"Shut up, Joseph," Maya said, glaring in his direction. "Now, Hudson, tell me, what is your schedule like this week?"

"I work day shift Monday and Tuesday. I took my night shifts off, then I'd be on my days off."

When I looked over at Maya, she had a huge grin on her face.

"Oh man, you walked right into that one," Joe said, leaning forward, getting ready to watch what was coming next. "She only gets that grin when she has an idea."

I looked over to see her still standing there with that Cheshire cat grin on her face. "Why do you look like that? You're freaking me out."

"Gah, this couldn't be more perfect!" she said, coming up and tapping me on the cheeks before delivering what I called her death pinch. "I love how my brain works."

"How so?" I asked, picking up my beer.

"Because I have a date for you on Thursday night."

As the words left her lips, the beer I'd drank hit the back of my throat and I coughed.

Liam, Joe, and Dax turned their undivided attention between me and Maya.

"I don't think so," I gritted, trying to gasp for air.

"Come on. It's one night!" Maya cried.

"Yeah, Hudson, come on, it's one night," Joe mocked.

I shook my head.

"Come on, please!" Maya cried.

I shook my head again.

"Give me one good reason why," she said, crossing her arms and tapping her foot. I'd seen her pull this with Liam and Joe before and somehow she always ended up getting her way.

"Well, for one, I don't date," I said, tapping her nose with my finger.

"What is the matter with you?"

"Not a thing." I shrugged.

"I thought your job is to serve and protect."

I nodded. "Correct. When I'm on duty, that is my job. So, who am I protecting and serving? Is it both? Is this a job you are offering? If so, tell me how much you are paying."

She brought her finger to her lips and stood there, staring off for a moment. "No, it's a date. You're paying." She crossed her arms over her chest.

"So, let me get this straight. My job is to serve and protect, however, this isn't a job. I'm being told to go on a date and that I'm paying. No thanks."

Maya stood there, scowling at me as Liam chuckled. She whipped around and looked at Liam, who automatically quieted down.

"Look, Hudson, Maya has a way of getting what she wants. So, you may as well cave now, otherwise I'm going to have to start on you. I don't want that."

I ran my hand through my hair. This Sunday had been going so well until she'd walked in. Who the hell gave her a key to this apartment? I didn't date, hadn't in a long time, and I liked it that way.

"Please," she said.

I let out a huff. "Who is it?"

"I'll tell you if you agree to go."

I gave her my highly disappointed look and then let out the breath I was holding. I'd been defeated. "Fine."

Maya looked around the room at all of us. "All of you heard that, correct?" she questioned, looking at all the guys.

Each one of them nodded, then gave me an apologetic look.

"Listen, no one breathes a word of this. It's supposed to be a blind date. Well, the other half thinks it's a blind date with someone she doesn't know. I need sworn promises from all of you."

"Fine," Joe answered.

"Yep," Liam said. "I don't need to be cut off."

"I'll do my best," Dax replied.

"No, Dax, you will shut it. Lock it up and throw it away," Maya said.

"Yep," he agreed.

"It's Bexley."

I frowned. What the hell would she need to be sent on a blind date for? She was smart, funny, attractive as hell, although in recent months she hadn't been around too much. The last few times I'd seen her, she'd been sad, almost as if she'd changed overnight.

"Isn't she…" It was then I remembered that she'd made me promise not to say anything, and although a lot of time had passed since that night, I still couldn't out her.

Maya just looked at me and shook her head.

I frowned. Had Maya known she was seeing some-one? Probably it was the way girls were.

Well, we'd be the perfect match—both sad, because deep down inside I was like that too, only I never showed it. Two broken people spending time together.

"Fine, send me the details."

"Yep, no worries. I'll text them over as soon as I figure them out."

CHAPTER FOUR

Bexley

I THOUGHT about how I really wanted to kill Maya as I stood in front of the mirror looking at myself. I'd tried on three different outfits and, at this moment, I didn't know why I even cared what I looked like. I also didn't know why or how I'd even agreed to doing this, but then Maya had that way about her.

I'd left brunch on Sunday, and by Monday night she'd messaged with a day and a time and told me my blind date would pick me up. For some reason or another, I didn't tell her no, probably because I knew if I had, she'd have driven over here and wouldn't have left until I'd said yes. She'd have brought reinforcements too, and I hadn't been in the mood for company.

I gave myself a once-over again and walked away from my reflection. There was no use worrying about tonight. I already knew it was going to end up on the huge list of regrets I already had. So what the hell was one more to add to an ever-growing list?

I made my way out to my living room and went to sit down and finish my lukewarm tea when someone knocked on the door. I glanced at my watch. There was no way that was my blind date. It was almost twenty-five minutes too early.

Another knock. "Coming!" I yelled, running to the door.

I opened the door and was surprised to see Hudson.

"Hey, detective." I smirked. "I'm getting ready to leave. What's up?" I questioned.

It wasn't unusual for Hudson to drop by while he was on duty. He used to bring a coffee often, and we'd hang out while he was on break. Although the frequency had stopped after that night in January, and it was even less now since I'd been punishing myself for that accident.

"What makes you think I'm on duty?" he asked, his eyes skimming my body.

I glanced down at myself, taking in the short, form-fitting black dress I'd chosen to wear, wondering if something was out of place.

"Um, hello, did you just plan on wearing a dark suit today?" I giggled.

"I don't wear this suit to work. It's my funeral suit. I'm here to pick you up for…. fuck it, Maya sent me."

He looked less than impressed, and I saw relief in his face after he told me Maya had sent him.

"Well, I'm honoured and bugged. I have a blind date with a guy wearing his funeral suit and I'm bugged with my so-called best friend! I sense this is going to be one hell of an evening. Let me grab my coat."

I heard Hudson chuckle as I grabbed my coat and purse, slipped my shoes on, and headed out the door with him.

Twenty minutes later, we sat inside The Harborview Courtyard looking over the menu.

"So, what made you decide to come here?" I questioned, looking around the room.

"Oh, Maya chose it." He sighed, closing the menu.

"Maya picked the restaurant?"

He took a sip of water and looked at me. "Well, she said you loved the place, so basically yes, she picked the restaurant." He smirked.

I nodded. "Right. Well, is there anything that you are picking?" I questioned.

"The tab. She told me I was to pick up the tab," he said, running his hand over his face.

To say this was awkward was an understatement. Not

that I didn't get along well with Hudson, I did, but I'd never looked at him as someone to date. We were friends. We'd only ever hung out alone when he'd stop by. Other than that, our friends always surrounded us.

"That's unfortunate because I didn't get to have lunch today, and she wasn't lying. This is my favourite restaurant."

"Okay, well then, I have one thing going for me. If this is your favorite place, then you can recommend something."

I smiled. "Sure can."

He picked up the menu and opened it up, placing it between us on the table. "I'm going to have the lobster bisque and a salad. They have the best lobster bisque I've ever had."

Hudson made a face. "You actually eat those?"

I giggled. "I do. Have you ever tried one?"

He nodded. "I have. I prefer my meat to come from the land, not the sea."

I couldn't help but laugh. "Okay, well then I'd say you need to try either the tenderloin or the New York strip. They are both equally amazing, and their double baked potatoes are to die for because, unlike other restaurants, they actually use real bacon and this cheese…god, I'm almost salivating just thinking about it."

"Here I thought you were drooling over me," Hudson said, a grin coming to his lips.

I couldn't help but laugh when I saw that smile.

"Okay there, handsome pants, you get to pick the appetizer." I winked.

His eyes landed on mine, and for the first time, I noticed just how blue they were.

"She called me handsome," he said, puffing out his chest.

I couldn't help but giggle as he finally tore his eyes from mine and looked down at the menu. "Okay, how about the cheddar and bacon pinwheels?"

I shook my head. "Those are disgusting. Try again."

He chuckled and glanced at the menu again. "Alright, how about the warm brie, with apple and pear?"

"Better choice." I smiled.

We both dug into the appetizer once it had been delivered to the table.

"Okay, you were right," Hudson said, his mouth full as he took the first bite. "This is to die for."

"Told you," I replied, my mouth full as well. "So tell me, how the hell you get roped into tonight?" I questioned, loading up another piece of garlic toast.

Hudson chuckled. "Well, you know Maya. She doesn't let up, and that sidekick of hers, well, he isn't any better."

I couldn't help but laugh. Hudson was right. Maya was unstoppable once she had an idea, always had been.

"Anyway, I don't mind. It's turning out to be a good night, with wonderful company." He winked.

My cheeks heated as I took another bite of that sinful appetizer. I listened to Hudson talk about Maya's ambush, laughing at almost everything he said. It was the first time in months I'd felt this light. It was a welcome feeling and one I wasn't sure I wanted to have end.

When my soup and salad was done, I sat there and watched as Hudson still worked on his New York strip.

"You still hungry?" he questioned.

"No, why?" I said, shaking my head.

"Because you look like you might attack my plate. The soup and salad looked more like appetizer size than meal size." Without another word, he cut the rest of his steak and potato in half and placed them on his slide plate.

"What are you doing?" I questioned.

He placed the plate in front of me. "Eat up." He winked.

I'd never had a date do anything like that before.

"Seriously, eat. You were right about these potatoes. To die for." He smiled, passing his knife to me so I could cut everything.

"Will there be anything else tonight?" the server asked as she cleared our plates. "Dessert?"

"Sure, please bring us a dessert menu," Hudson said, glancing over at me.

Once again, he placed the menu between us and asked me what was good. As I ran down the menu, I noticed immediately they'd brought back my favorite dessert, Sex in a Pan.

"Oh my gosh, we have to get this," I said, pointing to the item.

Hudson cocked his eyebrow as he read the menu and looked at me. "Are you trying to get me into bed?" he questioned, looking serious.

I let out a loud laugh, then covered my mouth as people turned to look at us, my cheeks heating. "No."

"Thank god, because I don't do that sort of thing on a first date." He chuckled. "Coffee?"

"Yes, please."

Soon, coffee and two pieces of Sex in a Pan were delivered to our table. One bite and we both closed our eyes as the sweet dessert hit our mouths.

"Here I thought you were crazy, suggesting that dessert, but I can seriously say I know where the name comes from." He chuckled.

"I know. It's like a full-blown orgasm with each bite," I answered.

"Is it now?" he asked, his face turning serious. "I wouldn't take it that far."

"It absolutely is."

Hudson shook his head. "I hate to say it, but I was right. You've been missing out, my dear. While it was good, I wouldn't take it that far."

For the first time tonight, my mind actually wandered to that place. Our conversation flashed through my mind, the one we'd had that night in January. I remembered the look on his face as Id approached him, asking if there was someone he knew of that could do better than that guy I'd been seeing. Then I wondered if he'd been talking about himself. What would it be like to be with Hudson, something I'd never even thought of? I shook the thought from my head. I wasn't sure why I was even thinking about that. Maybe it was the alcohol we'd had with dinner.

"What are you thinking about?" he asked, bringing me back into the moment.

I shook my head. "Nothing."

Hudson picked up the dessert menu again and then looked at me. "Want to split something else?"

"Sure," I answered, not believing the amount of food we'd already consumed.

WE'D STOPPED for a coffee on our way from the restaurant and had parked down by the water before Hudson drove me home.

"Sorry, had I have planned this date, I'd have thought of something to do after dinner." He shrugged.

"It's okay. I'm sure you probably weren't all that thrilled with Maya's idea to begin with."

"Why would you say that?" he asked, passing me my coffee.

"Because I know Maya well, and I know her idea's well. That mind of hers can be frightening."

"Well, that is true. Don't put yourself down, though, and to let you know, I had a good time tonight."

I looked over at him. He didn't look at me; he just stared out the front window of the car at the lake.

"Same here," I said, looking out the front window.

We sat in silence. He was acting funny, and it made me on edge. This wasn't the normal Hudson. Normally, he would crack some joke about something. Instead, he'd grown oddly serious after he admitted to having a good time tonight.

"So had you planned tonight, what would we be doing right now?"

When I looked over, he jerked his head away and looked out the driver's side window. He probably didn't think I'd seen him watching me, but I had. "Well?"

"I might have taken you down to that little carnival

on the outskirts of town. You know that one that sucks all your money before they allow you to win anything?"

"Really?" I asked.

"Not into carnival games?"

"I didn't say that. What else?"

"After I won you a bear, I'd have brought you here and we could have walked through the park, hand-in-hand, maybe sat at the water's edge for a bit or taken a swim."

I looked out toward the water and smiled. "Well, what are you waiting for?"

He looked over at me and frowned.

"Let's go for that walk."

We walked for a bit before taking a seat on one of the picnic tables in the park. Hudson surprised me by not sitting beside me but climbing up and sitting on the top of the picnic table, straddling my body. It was when I felt his large hands on my shoulders I wondered what was going on. I said nothing, I just sat there waiting to see what he was going to do.

I closed my eyes as he began rubbing my shoulders, then digging his fingers into my neck. I let out a sigh and felt my body relax as he continued.

"Feel okay?" he murmured.

"Mmmmyes." I half moaned, enjoying the feel of his hands on me.

An hour later, we arrived back at his truck. He

opened the door for me and then drove me home. I went up to my apartment alone, and once inside, I quickly changed, made a cup of tea, and then went into the living room and flopped onto the couch, turning on the TV.

I had such a great time tonight. Hudson was completely different on his own, and whatever had happened between him telling me he'd had a good time and him dropping me off had me hoping that he'd asked me out again sometime soon.

CHAPTER FIVE

Hudson

I'D WOKEN over an hour ago but was still lying in bed, my arm behind my head, my phone in my hand. I stared down at the message I'd typed out, debating if I should change anything before I sent it. My finger hovered over the button, but then quickly hit delete instead. Then my phone vibrated. First it was Dax, then Tate, and then Liam. I knew it was only going to be a matter of minutes before Joe chimed in.

I threw the covers off and got up out of bed, heading to the shower. I'd had plans to send that message for days, but each time I'd type out the same thing, and then

I'd sit and stare at the words I'd written, then I'd delete it.

I got dressed, grabbed a protein shake from the cupboard, shoved my phone in my pocket, and took off out the door. I was late for our pool game this morning.

I'd done nothing but try to stop thinking about that date the other night. It was odd I'd even given it another thought, to be honest. I didn't date. I'd convinced myself over the years I didn't need anyone, yet here I was wondering what it would be like to have someone in my life, a significant other, once again. I just hoped I'd healed enough to take something like that on again.

I shoved the door open and walked into Joe's, slipped my shoes off, and made my way to where the boys were. I stepped into the room and almost immediately, my eyes landed on Maya. She sat on Liam's lap on the couch, her arms around his neck, while Tate and Dax played pool.

"It's about time you got here," Joe said, coming in from outside with some drinks in his hand. We'd set up a bar fridge out on the back deck for our fire pit nights. It had made Everly happy to have her fridge back again.

"Yes, it is," Maya said, getting up off Liam's lap and coming around the table.

"Since when do you play pool with us on guys' day?" I questioned.

"Since I want to know how that date went the other night," she said, crossing her arms in front of her chest.

When all eyes turned to me, I wondered what the hell I'd done to fuck it up. I could feel the tension pouring off Maya and knew she was going to blame me for something.

"What do you want to know?" I questioned, not backing down.

"How was it?"

I looked over her shoulder to see all the guys now watching us. Talk about feeling ambushed. The guys had asked about my blind date, but I'd just shrugged and said it went fine.

"It was fine."

Maya shook her head. "Fine…only fine?"

I nodded, not sure what it was she was wanted me to say. I'd gone on one date. What answer was she expecting? Then I remembered Bexley commenting about how Maya's mind worked, and I chuckled to myself.

"Is that why you didn't call her yet?" she questioned, placing her hands on her hips.

From the corner of my eye, I caught Tate whispering something to Liam and Liam nodding his head. I couldn't imagine what he'd said, but when I looked back at Maya, I could see the anger on her face. Why the hell was she angry at me? I'd done what she'd asked, I'd taken her on the date.

I could feel sweat forming on my brow. I shrugged. "I didn't know I was supposed to follow up," I answered, feeling the wrath of Maya coming down on me at any moment.

Suddenly, she was right in my face. "You didn't *know*? How the hell did you not know to follow up with her? Isn't there some sort of written word that you at least follow up and make sure they have a good time?"

I glanced over my shoulder at Liam, who sat there and shrugged his shoulders. Wasn't he going to help me? Then I looked over at Joe, who did the same.

"Don't look at them," Maya gritted. "Why didn't you call her?"

I pulled at the collar of my T-shirt then smiled. "It wasn't because I didn't want to call. It was more because I didn't know what to say. I asked her the night of the date and she said she had a good time," I murmured, really feeling the pressure right now. "I'm sorry. I'm just really rusty at this dating thing."

"Rusty? Rusty?" Maya said, her voice getting more high-pitched the second time around.

"Yes, rusty," I admitted.

"Well, do something about it, would you? I can't stand to see my friend this upset!" she yelled, leaving the room.

Immediately, Liam stood up and took off after her, leaving us alone.

"What the hell is with your sister?" I questioned, looking over at Joe.

He was quiet for a moment, then he looked at me and shrugged his shoulders. "Don't mess up her plans for great things."

I WALKED into the emergency department carrying a single red rose and approached the main desk. Bexley worked around here somewhere. I just didn't know exactly where. A woman sat behind the desk typing away on the computer. It took her a minute, but she finally looked up from the screen she was staring at and smiled.

"Can I help you?"

"I'm looking for Bexley Andrews."

"Ah, yes. She just ran some files down to the other desk. She should be back soon. Why don't you take a seat over there?" she said, smiling.

I nodded and made my way over to the bank of chairs and turned to sit down when I saw Bexley come around the corner talking with another girl. She'd just made it to the desk when she looked up and over at me.

I lifted my hand, waved, and smiled.

Her expression told me instantly she was surprised to see me. I'd only ever run into her one other time, and that was when I brought someone in for a psych evaluation. She finished her conversation, and I stood up as she made her way over to me.

"Hudson? What are you doing here?" she asked, grabbing hold of my jacket and pulling me into the corner away from the prying eyes of the other nurses.

"I um…" I glanced down at the rose in my hand and held it out for her to take. "I wanted to apologize for being so rusty. I should have called you, but I didn't know what to say. So, I think it's best if we go on another date. That way, I can make it up to you."

"By taking me on a pity date?" She frowned, taking the flower from my hand and bringing it to her nose. "Did Maya put you up to this?"

I frowned, unsure of how to answer her. When she looked up at me, I could see laughter in her eyes.

"Relax, I was only kidding. Although, not about the Maya part. I can see her forcing you to do something like this," she said, looking up at me as she smelled the rose again.

I smiled. "Well, if you want to look at it as a pity date, it would be you taking pity on me, not the other way around."

She smelled the rose again. "This is really beautiful."

"I hoped you'd like it."

She nodded, a small smile coming to her lips. "I really do. It's simple, to the point, and beautiful."

"Sort of like you. Those purple scrubs you have on

bring out the colour in your eyes," I said, knocking her shoulder with mine.

Instantly, her cheeks flushed, and she averted her eyes from mine.

"Do you have a break soon?"

She nodded, meeting my eyes. "In ten minutes."

"Okay, how about I meet you in the cafeteria? We can talk about our next date." I winked.

Once again, she smiled. "Sounds good."

CHAPTER SIX

Bexley

SLIPPING FROM BED, I headed toward the shower. It had been a long week at work, and I was glad it was over. The only part that had made it pleasant was Hudson. Ever since he'd shown up and brought me that rose, he'd made a point of coming by and spending my lunch hour with me.

We'd had lunch in the cafeteria on the days it had rained, and outside on the days it hadn't. He'd even surprised me with a hot picnic lunch one afternoon. The last couple days I'd worked the night shift, but that hadn't stopped him. Instead of coming by, he'd called me during my lunch hour and we'd FaceTimed. I was seeing a different side of him, one I knew I'd get used to if I allowed myself to. Then, before we'd gotten off the phone last night, he'd asked me out on a date tonight. I didn't normally do anything on my first night off, but I agreed anyway.

Halfway through the last part of my shift, I started coming down with the chills, so I ended up coming home a little earlier than expected and crawled right into bed. I was still feeling run down as I turned the shower on, letting it warm up before stepping in.

Once inside, I let the hot water run down my body. Hudson was picking me up around six and we were going to see a movie at the local theatre. I'd been so happy when he'd insisted on picking me up, even though I'd offered to meet him there. I hated driving at night now, so much so I'd started taking the bus to the hospital when I had to work nights. It added an extra forty minutes to the beginning and end of my shift, but that was fine with me.

Forty minutes later, we stood in the movie theatre waiting to get popcorn. Hudson seemed on edge.

"I forgot to tell you that you look nice," Hudson said as he looked up at the menu behind the counter.

I looked over at him. I could see the tension in his face and in his shoulders. He hadn't been like that at all during the week, which made me question if Maya wasn't hiding somewhere.

I glanced down at myself. I was wearing my favorite pair of ripped jeans and a black long-sleeved blouse, something he'd seen me in a million times before but had said nothing.

"Thanks. I'm glad to see you in something other than your funeral suit."

Hudson chuckled. "You'll have to forgive me for that. Like I say, I really suck at this dating thing."

"I'll be the judge of that," I replied.

"You will?"

"I will."

We both took a step forward when it was our turn. Hudson ordered an extra-large popcorn and two pops, then looked over at me. "Did you want candy?"

"How did you guess?" I questioned, wondering if Maya had mentioned something to him about my love for something sweet and salty.

"I guessed?" He shrugged. "Grab whatever you want."

Immediately, I reached for the chocolate M&M's and placed them on the counter beside the popcorn.

"Good choice," he said, pulling his wallet from his back pocket.

I WIPED my eyes as the credits rolled. The ending of the movie was incredibly sad, and while I wasn't one to cry at movies, this one had hit home.

We sat there as the theatre emptied. Once the last person exited the theatre, I went to get up, but Hudson shook his head, grabbed my hand, and pulled me back down to my seat.

"Let's just wait here. We can finish the popcorn?" he said, picking up the bag and waving it in front of me, making me laugh as he pulled it away just as I went to grab some.

I shoved my hand in the bag, taking a handful. Then I sat back against the seat. "What did you think of the movie?"

"It was good, a little slow, but that ending grabbed me. What about you?"

"Same," he said, meeting my eyes. "Not enough to shed tears, though," he whispered as his thumb wiped away a stray tear from my cheek.

He passed the bag again, and I took another handful. Once the music from the credits ended, the room grew quiet. I relaxed back against the seat and shoved more popcorn into my mouth, taking in the quietness.

"I don't think I've ever stayed inside a theatre until it emptied. This is sort of fun and weird at the same time. It's so quiet."

Hudson looked over at me and smiled. "I used to do this all the time as a kid, more to cause shit than anything else," he said, raising his eyebrows.

I giggled again. "I could see that about you."

"Are you saying I'm a troublemaker?" he asked with a look of shock and disbelief.

"If the shoe fits." I shrugged.

Hudson's jaw dropped, and he reached over and playfully grabbed my side, causing me to scream.

"Why are you screaming?" he questioned, doing it once again, making me laugh hard.

I let out a shrill scream before laughing as he continued to tickle me. I pushed at his hands, but it did little good. He had me, and I was losing strength from laughing so hard. Finally, once I was breathless, he stopped and sat back.

"Let that be a lesson to you. I'm not a troublemaker," he whispered into my ear.

We heard a door open and then shut, and soon a couple of teenagers appeared carrying brooms and garbage bags.

I glanced at Hudson, but he shook his head and held his finger over his lips.

"Sir, excuse me, sir. Miss. Sorry, but you are going to have to leave so we can clean the theatre," I young attendant said.

"Oh, really?" Hudson questioned.

"Yes, sir."

I grabbed his hand and went to stand up, but he didn't move.

"But the movie is going to start?" Hudson said, causing me to laugh. "We can't stay and wait."

The kid shook his head, climbing the stairs toward us. "You shouldn't even have been allowed in if it's for the next viewing."

"Come on," I said, pulling on his hand.

"Oh, they told us to come on in and sit down. That it was fine. So we are going to wait here."

The young kid looked over his shoulder at his friend. "Sir, if you won't leave, I'm going to be forced to call theatre security."

"Is that really a thing?" Hudson questioned, giving me the side-eye and winking.

"I'm afraid it is, sir."

Hudson chuckled and finally got up, slipped his hand in mine, and we walked to the end of the aisle.

"Sorry about that. I was only playing around." He

grinned at the kid. "Shouldn't take your job so seriously."

As we made our way down the stairs toward the door, I leaned in and whispered, "For a police officer, you get into a lot of trouble, don't you?"

Hudson shrugged. "Sometimes it's worth it." He winked. "I've always wondered what the secret is. Why we can't be in the theatre when they clean? Is there some secret club or something?"

I couldn't help but laugh the more I thought about what he'd said. "Must be. I guess we will never know," I replied as he slipped his hand into mine.

WE WALKED hand-in-hand through the empty parking lot of my building to the main door. Hudson waited while I slipped the key into the lock and stepped inside with me. I pressed the button for the elevator, and while we waited, I leaned against the wall and closed my eyes for a moment.

"I had a good time tonight," he breathed.

I opened my eyes and met his. "Me too," I whispered.

As we stood there waiting for the elevator, unspoken words passed between us. My heart beat hard, and I felt warm as he brought his hand to my cheek. He leaned in slowly and pressed a light kiss to my lips. He backed away, putting a little space between us. I could feel the heat from his body, warm and soothing. I wanted him to kiss me again. I wanted to feel his lips pressed against mine again.

I was just about to lean forward when the elevator opened.

"There's the elevator," he mumbled.

"There it is," I repeated.

We both stood there, neither of saying a word. When the elevator started to close, he stuck his hand in the door and stepped back, waiting for me to move. I pushed off the wall, and stepped inside, turning back to look at him. As the door started to close, I held my hand over the sensor, reached out and grabbed his shirt and pulled him inside. The world melted away as he forced me up against the elevator wall, pressed his body against mine, and took my mouth with his.

CHAPTER SEVEN

Hudson

THINGS HAD GOTTEN PRETTY HEATED between us the night we'd shared that kiss. However, I hadn't seen Bexley since I left. We'd both been working opposite shifts too, so the only way we'd spoken was through text message, until last night. I'd FaceTimed with her from the cruiser while I took some time to have a coffee and a sandwich. It had been the best part of my week since that night.

Tonight was our third date. I was looking forward to it. I actually couldn't wait to see her, which was why I'd called her last night.

I walked into the changing room and went to my locker. Joe, Tate, Dax, and Liam all sat there, wrapped in a towel after their showers, talking away about our guys' night out, which was coming up next Friday.

"'Bout time you got here," Joe said.

I shook my head. "Some of us had paperwork to finish," I muttered as my phone vibrated against my locker.

"Paperwork...there is always time for paperwork," Joe kidded.

Ignoring him, I grabbed my phone and checked my messages. My heart raced at the sight of Bexley's name.

BEXLEY: What time are we meeting up?

Hudson: I'll pick you up at 7

Bexley: See you then. Where are we going again?

Hudson: Thought we'd go for dinner at that restaurant you'd suggested.

I WATCHED for a sign of a reply, but there was nothing. I frowned as I waited. We'd been texting on and off all day, and she'd been answering me almost immediately.

. . .

Hudson: If you'd prefer somewhere else, just say so.

Bexley: No, it's fine.

Hudson: Okay, see you soon.

I grabbed the large towel I'd thrown into my bag this morning along with my toiletry bag I kept in my locker and headed to the showers. Twenty minutes later, I emerged, hoping the guys would be gone by now, but no such luck. They now sat around half-dressed, still talking about Friday.

"Don't you guys have places to be?" I questioned, feeling somewhat annoyed that they were still here.

"Everly works late tonight at the office," Joe replied.

"Maya is with her parents at the summer festival. I'm supposed to meet them for dinner in an hour. We leave for the bed-and-breakfast tomorrow." Liam shrugged.

Then I looked over to Dax and Tate, who both smiled. "What about you?" They asked in unison.

I pulled out a fresh pair of jeans and a black button-down shirt from my locker and hung them on the door.

"That's a pretty nice outfit just to go home in, Hudson. You got a date?" Dax asked.

This was why I wished they'd left. I knew they were going to bust my balls about tonight. I'd kept pretty quiet about things with Bexley. Of course the guys knew I'd taken her on more than one date, but they didn't know about the lunches, or about the kiss.

"The lack of response tells me you two hit the nail on the head." Liam chuckled.

I glanced over my shoulder and glared at him.

"If the four of you must know, yes, Bexley and I are heading for dinner tonight."

The room was quiet, and then Joe spoke.

"Wait, isn't this, what, your third date?" Joe questioned, locking his locker and slipping into his jacket.

"Why, I believe you are right there, Joe. It would be their third date," Liam added.

"Wow, our boy is growing up." Tate chuckled. "Third date, that is a big step."

Frowning, I turned around and looked at the four of them. The only one who hadn't added anything was Dax.

"Don't you have anything to say about it?" I questioned, looking at him.

Dax shook his head, as the room quieted. I'd just turned back to my locker when I heard him speak. "Only that the third date normally means you are going to get laid."

I whipped back around in time to catch him with a huge grin on his face.

My eyes were glued on Dax, until one of them shoved a condom in my face. I reached out and took the condom from whoever held onto it and turned to see Tate with laughter in his eyes.

"What the fuck, bro?"

"Hey…one can't be too safe, and honestly, you should be well protected while you serve. Think of it as a bulletproof vest for the lil guy."

The rest of them burst out into laughter while I stood there. "You are all sick. You know that?"

"We know." They all laughed and took off out of the changing room to leave me in peace.

I PULLED into the parking lot of her apartment building and parked my car in the visitors' section and made my way up to her place. Traffic had been a nightmare, and thanks to the guys giving me a hard time, I was later than I wanted to be. I knocked on her door and stood back, waiting for her to answer.

After a few minutes, I knocked again, this time a little harder, and finally heard movement on the other side of the door. When the door opened, Bexley stood in front of me looking a little pale and ringing her hands together.

"Hey." I smiled. "You okay?"

Only she didn't smile back. She didn't even answer me. She just moved to the side and signalled for me to come in. Once inside, I slipped my shoes off and looked at her.

"Everything okay?" I questioned again. "I'm sorry I'm a little late."

It wasn't like Bexley to be upset at the fact someone was late, so I didn't know why I even apologized. I'd known her long enough to know she wasn't that uptight.

"It's, um…it's been a long day," she said, breathing a little harder than normal. She made her way to the living room and sat down on the couch.

I walked in and looked at her. Something was wrong. She seemed off.

"What's going on?" I questioned, taking a seat in the chair across from her. I didn't want to crowd her. She looked like she was on the edge of a breakdown, and I wanted her to talk to me.

"Sorry, this is something I don't let on, but I'm having a bit of an anxiety attack here. I actually wasn't even going to open the door," she said, placing her hand on her chest and closing her eyes.

"Would you like some water?" I asked.

She looked around the room and nodded. Immediately, I made my way to the kitchen and pulled out a bottle of water from the fridge and made my way back to her, opening it as I went. I watched as she reached out with shaking hands and took the water, bringing it to her lips and taking a drink.

"What got you upset?" I questioned.

She shrugged. "I guess it was just the day."

She sat there quietly, holding onto the water, staring at the floor.

"Would you prefer not to go tonight? We can order in instead, put a movie on and curl up on the couch together if you like."

Her eyes flew to mine, and she looked at me as if she hadn't heard what I'd said. I was about to repeat my question when she cleared her throat. "Are you sure?"

I nodded. "I want to make sure you are comfortable. If there is one thing I've learned, it's that people with anxiety need safe surroundings. Not that you aren't ever safe with me, but you need to feel comfortable. So, how about a pizza?" I questioned.

"Hmmm, I'd die for pizza from Cosmo's," Bexley muttered, still shaking as she took another drink.

I stood up and took my hoodie off. It had been surprisingly cool for a summer night, and I'd been glad I'd had it. Without a thought, I wrapped it around her, then I pulled up the website for the pizza place while I watched her slip her arms into my sweater and wrap it around her.

"Okay, let's see. Do you want the usual?" I questioned.

We'd ordered pizza so many times, I could recite her order by heart. Double cheese and mushrooms. Sometimes, she wanted pepperoni, but most times not.

She nodded. "Double cheese and mushrooms," she muttered, pulling my sweater around her more.

"No worries, I got you." I winked.

I placed our order, and when I hung up, I'd noticed she was watching me. "What is it?"

"You actually remembered my pizza order without me having to tell you, didn't you?"

I nodded and smiled. "I did. Now, scoot over. Let's pick something to watch."

She moved over and reached for the remote and started up Netflix; we surfed around, each of us picking a movie before the pizza came. I tossed a coin into the air and let her call it, before we dug into the mouthwatering pizza. *Eat Pray Love* it was.

I LAY ON THE COUCH, on my back, arm over my head, almost asleep by the time the credits rolled. Bexley had settled in beside me, thrown a blanket over herself, and had curled into me.

"Feeling better?" I asked, pulling her against me.

"Much." She rested her chin on her hand so she could look at me.

"Good." I brushed a strand of hair from her face. "I'll admit I was worried when I got here. I don't think I've ever seen you like that."

She shrugged. "It happens sometimes," she whispered, hiding her eyes from me. "It's a little embarrassing to me. I'm still trying to deal with it."

"It's alright, Bex, it doesn't make me love you any less." I winked.

She smiled as she met my eyes. I couldn't help but study her. She was beautiful. It surprised me I'd never noticed it before. I pulled her against me and pressed my lips to hers. I'd been dying to do this all night, ever since I'd walked through the door, but hadn't wanted to upset her in her current state. She shifted in my arms as our kiss deepened.

My tongue parted her lips, and I heard a soft moan escape as I ran my tongue against hers. I shifted a bit and raised up on my forearm, bringing my free hand to her cheek to deepen our kiss even more. I loved kissing her.

An hour later, we stood in one another's arms at the

door to her place. We hadn't been able to break our kiss even for a moment. I gripped her ass, pulling her against me as I kissed her hard. My cock was hard as a rock, and I needed relief.

"God…" she muttered as our lips finally parted.

"What?" I asked, as I kissed my way down her neck.

She took my hand and placed it on her breast. I could feel her nipple through her shirt. I ran my thumb over the hardened nub, while meeting her lips. Pinching it gently through her shirt, I heard her make a throaty groan.

"You like that?"

"Do it again," she whispered, her breath tickling my ear.

I did as she asked, a little harder this time, and I felt her fist my shirt. I closed my eyes for a second and sucked in a breath as she ran her hand over my cock for the first time. Waves of pleasure and want raced through me.

I looked into her eyes. I could see the want in them.

"Want to go to the bedroom?" I murmured, afraid that if I said the wrong thing, or if she wasn't ready, this would all end.

I watched as her cheeks flushed, then she bit her bottom lip, hid her eyes from mine, and nodded. She tugged on my arm, pulling me toward her bedroom.

We wasted no time. The second that door was closed, she was already tugging at the buttons on my shirt and then at the button of my jeans, while I did the same to her. Seconds later, we crashed into one another, falling to the bed.

I rolled up onto my arms, kissing her, as my hands explored her body. I kissed my way to her breasts, sucking one nipple into my mouth, wagging my tongue over it, before moving to the other. Her soft moans were like music to my ears, and when I slid my hand between her legs, she let out the sexiest moan I'd ever heard.

A few passes over her clit, I could feel her body start to shake. She was ready. I reached for my jeans that were on the floor, but she stopped me.

"What are you doing?" she asked, breathing hard.

"I was going to grab the con—"

She pressed her fingers to my lips and shyly shook her head. "No condom."

"Bex... I..."

"No condom. I want to feel you inside me. You, not something between us."

She pressed her lips to mine and took my cock in her hand, stroking me. She straddled my lap and lined me up at her opening, then interlaced her fingers with mine as she slid onto me. The moan that escaped her lips sent waves through me. I loved how responsive she was to sex. I gripped her hips as she rode me and watched as she grabbed her breasts, gently pinching her nipples. I sat up, held her to me, and kissed each of them, before sliding out of her and placing her on the bed. I stood up, coming up behind her.

I gently pressed onto her back, gripped her hip, and slid myself deep inside of her from behind. Fisting my fingers into her thick hair, I gently tugged, immediately feeling her pussy clench around me.

"Reach down and rub your clit," I whispered in her ear as I tugged gently on her hair.

I felt her hand move and her body writhe as I pumped into her.

CHAPTER EIGHT

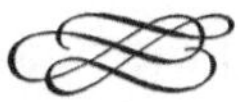

Bexley

I COULD FEEL my orgasm building and it was becoming too hard to hold back. I'd never been one to like having my hair pulled, it felt like they were trying to dominate me, but with Hudson, it felt different—safe.

"Stop rubbing," he demanded. "I don't want you to come just yet," he whispered in my ear.

He stopped moving, let go of my hair, and just waited, his hard cock throbbing deep inside of me. I finally regained control of my breathing and, just as I did, I felt his hands reach around and cup my breasts, the weight of them resting in his hands as he stroked my nipples. He pulled me up, so I was kneeling on the bed, his cock still planted deep inside of me, and kissed me hard.

"You ready to come now?" he whispered, his lips against mine.

I nodded as he kissed me again, slower this time.

"How about you get on your back?" he whispered, pulling himself from me.

I lay down and moved up a little, while Hudson knelt down on the bed. He ran his hands up my leg, then gripped my foot, bringing my ankle to his lips. Slowly, he kissed his way up my leg, then my hip, my tummy, between my breasts, until he met my mouth.

Parting my legs around him, he slid himself into me, holding me, kissing me as he slowed his pace. My fingers dug into his back muscles the closer I got. Every nerve in my body was on fire. He held me tight as we both came.

I'D BEEN awake for the better part of an hour, staring up at the ceiling, while Hudson snored softly beside me. The memory of last night was vivid, and my body hurt in places it hadn't in a long time.

I slipped from the bed and hopped in the shower. I'd felt more alive today than I had in months. Once showered, I decided to surprise him with breakfast. I got right to it, first frying the bacon while getting the eggs ready to be scrambled. I'd just dumped the eggs onto the plates and turned to place them on the table when I caught movement out of the corner of my eye.

I whipped around to see Hudson leaning against the doorframe. He was already dressed. His jeans hung low on his hips and his shirt lay over the back of the chair. He stood there, watching me, a small smile on his face.

"God, you scared me." I giggled.

His eyes ran the length of my body. I looked down at myself. I'd gotten out of the shower and realized my clothes were in the bedroom. I hadn't wanted to disturb Hudson, so I had thrown on his hoodie and nothing else.

"I borrowed it. Is that okay?" I questioned.

He nodded. Taking a step into the kitchen, he grabbed his shirt and pulled me into him. "Good morning," he whispered as he wrapped his arms around me. He slowly brought his lips to mine. "Would have been nice to wake up with you beside me," he said, kissing me again.

"Oh, I wanted to surprise you," I whispered, nodding to the two plates on the counter. "I made us breakfast."

I slid from his arms and brought over the plates, placing them on the table. I grabbed the two glasses of juice I'd poured and brought them over, then sat down beside him. He'd already dug into the eggs.

"I don't think I've ever had anyone make me breakfast before."

"Does everything taste okay?" I asked, taking a bite of my bacon.

Hudson nodded. "What about you?"

"Bacon is good. Haven't tried the eggs yet. Sometimes, I over cook them." I shrugged.

He looked at me. "I wasn't talking about breakfast."

I felt my cheeks heat. I knew he was going to ask me about last night. Two people who have been friends for a while and then sleep together normally don't ever work out. I was worried about that. We hung in the same circle. What would it be like if we decided we weren't for one another?

"Be honest," he added.

"Honest?" I asked.

"Yes, honest."

I was quiet for a moment as all these thoughts and feelings ran through me. I took a drink of juice to get rid of the dry spot at the back of my throat. "It was amazing," I said, my voice cracking. "What about me, was I okay?"

I could feel my cheeks heating as I waited for his response.

He met my eyes. "You were more than amazing," he said, leaning in and kissing me.

He dug his fork back into his eggs.

"Can I tell you something else?" I questioned.

"Of course."

"I never thought I'd date again, nor get laid again."

Hudson broke out into laughter. "Why's that?"

February was something I hadn't spoken about with any of my friends, aside from Maya. It hurt way too much, and all I'd wanted to do was forget it. I'd done well, I'd ignored what had happened, and I'd holed up in my apartment using excuse upon excuse to keep my friends away, until now. Until Maya had set Hudson and me up.

"I didn't tell anyone." I swallowed hard.

"What? Did you have a nasty breakup or something?" Hudson asked. "Did the guy not give you the big O?"

"No. You know I have dated no one seriously since last summer, and the guy in January doesn't count. We never made it more than a few dates."

"Okay, so what is it?"

I looked down at my plate. "In February, Valentine's Day, to be exact, I was working out of town at a hospital. I'd been sent to cover a few shortages during the night shift. We got everything caught up ,and since I had put in so much overtime, I left a few hours early and made my home. I was driving down this country road when suddenly, out of nowhere, there was a person. I swerved but couldn't avoid him."

I looked up to see the shock on Hudson's face. "Oh my god, Bex, why didn't you say anything to any of us?"

"I only told Maya." I shrugged. "Anyway, I rushed out of the car and ran over to him. He was in bad shape, mangled from being hit, but he was talking. Then suddenly he wasn't breathing. I ran and got my first-aid kit and my phone, calling the police and ambulance while I went to work on him. His girlfriend stood at the side of the road, crying. I did everything I could, everything I'd been trained to do, but couldn't save him. By the time the paramedics arrived, he was gone."

I picked up my glass and took a drink, clearing the hard lump that sat in my throat.

"When the police got there, they talked to his girlfriend and then told me there would be no charges. I do not know why. I mean, I hit him and he died. I didn't see him, and I just can't forgive myself. I can still hear his girlfriend crying, screaming at the police."

I wiped my eyes, feeling the overwhelming sadness taking over once again.

When I looked over at Hudson, he had a funny look on his face. One I hadn't seen before. He dragged his fork through his eggs, then stood up. He looked like he was going to be sick, and instantly I grew worried. "Look, I've got to get going," he muttered.

I frowned. I'd opened up like he'd asked. Had I said something wrong? "You're leaving?" I questioned.

He said nothing. He just went to the door and shoved his feet into his shoes, opened the door, and left my apartment. I stood there, not sure what had happened, but I could already feel my world starting to crumble.

I'd opened up, probably way more than I should have. We never should have slept together. I'd been honest like he'd asked, and he'd been the first and only person, aside from Maya, that I'd told about that night and the one person I never thought would have left me, especially after everything that had happened last night. I walked into the living room, sat down on the couch, and burst into tears.

I'D SPENT the day wrapped in blankets on the couch. After Hudson left, I'd spent the next couple of hours crying. I didn't understand what I'd said or done to make him leave the way he did. I finally picked up the book I'd been reading and did everything I could to get lost in the pages. Anything to take my mind off the fact that he'd left. I was just about finished when my phone vibrated on the table.

Maya: You up for bowling?

Bexley: Nope

MY ANSWER WAS simple and to the point, which Maya didn't always like. However, I didn't want to be bothered. I didn't want to be asked questions about how our third date had gone. The girls would see right through me, that I knew.

Maya: Spending the night with Hudson?

Bexley: Nope

INSTANTLY, those three little dots jumped around. They looked more frantic than usual, and I could imagine Maya doing the same thing as she typed. I wasn't sure I even wanted to see what it was she was going to say. I placed my phone on my stomach and closed my eyes until I felt it vibrate.

Maya: What do you mean, nope.

Bexley: Exactly what I said.

Maya: What happened?

Bexley: I don't want to talk about it.

Maya: Too bad, you are going to talk about it.

Bexley: I'm not.

Maya: You are.

SUDDENLY, my phone started dinging, and I noticed both Poppy and Everly had been added to our chat. Talk about feeling ambushed. I let out a sigh.

Everly: What is going on?

Poppy: Looks like we've been added to a chat. See above.

Everly: Oh my, what is going on Bex?

Bexley: Nothing. I am just staying in okay. I want to be alone.

Maya: She is lying. There is something wrong. I can sense it.

Poppy: If she wants to stay in, let her. It doesn't mean anything is wrong.

Everly: Yeah really, sometimes we all need to have our own time. I'm a huge advocate of it.

Maya: Ugh, you two aren't listening to me. I'm telling you, something isn't right. Liam left to go over to Hudson's place. Said it was important but he wouldn't tell me why.

Poppy: I think you are jumping to conclusions. They are being guys. Maybe he needs help with a car repair or something. Or maybe they just want to drink beer in peace.

Maya: I'm telling you, something is going on.

> Bexley: Ugh. Can't you just leave it alone?

I THREW my phone on the couch and buried my face in my hands. I took a few deep breaths and picked my phone back up.

> Maya: I told you girls there was something wrong.

> Everly: Maybe she is just having a day. You were pretty grumpy the other day, according to Liam.

> Poppy: No, I'm going to have to agree with Maya. Something isn't right. She isn't normally this short. I'm worried.

> Maya: We should go to her place instead of bowling, find out what is going on.

> Everly: I'm not sure that is a good idea. This is the therapist talking now.

THAT WAS the last message on my phone. They'd been sent while I'd been trying to calm myself down. I did not know what was going on or if they were really going to show up at my door.

Bexley: Hello???

I WATCHED for any sign or a response, but there was nothing. It was like I was yelling into the void. I got up, slipped my feet into my slippers, and went to the kitchen to make some tea. I'd just gotten back to the couch when I heard a knock on my door. As I approached, I heard both Poppy and Everly talking away. I let out a breath and pulled the door open.

"What's going on?" I questioned.

"Maya sent us. Damage control," Everly said, coming in with an enormous bag of popcorn.

"I've got the chocolate," Poppy added, holding up two bags of my favorite candy-coated chocolate, which only reminded me of movie night.

Everly wrapped her arms around me before heading into the living room, and Poppy did the same. These two were going to make me break down, I just knew it. Once

they were inside, I shut and locked the door, then joined
them in the living room.

WHEN THEY'D FINALLY GOT me talking, there was no
turning back. I told them about the accident because that
was what had upset me the most. The fact that I'd told
Hudson something so personal, and something that had
harmed me as much as it had, only to have him walk out
on me, had devastated me. The entire time I sat there
sharing the story with them, I was worried that they
would do the same thing Hudson had.

When I finished, I wiped my cheeks. My chest hurt,
my eyes were red, I was a complete and utter mess.
Poppy and Everly looked at one another, and then Everly
reached over and took hold of my hand.

"Bex, you went through something very traumatic.
It's okay to be upset, and it's not a wonder you pulled
away from all of us. Are you sure you didn't read into his
leaving? That perhaps he hadn't gotten a text about
something and had to leave?"

"I was sitting right there. He never touched his phone."

"You realize that when you were telling us about the

accident that you never actually looked at either of us? Are you certain you didn't do the same thing with him?"

I thought for a moment. This was why I never talked about this accident, because when I had to, I blanked every time. I'd done it with Maya, and I'd done it with the doctor I'd seen at the hospital who had prescribed me sleeping pills shortly after it happened because I hadn't been able to sleep. When I'd walked from that appointment, he'd also given me a referral to see a psychiatrist. I could remember being pissed off about it at the time, but perhaps Everly was on to something.

"I don't think so. I mean, he was right beside me. I'm sure I would have noticed."

"You didn't notice when we offered you popcorn or these little delights," Everly said, holding up the bag of candy.

I frowned. Had I really blacked out? I could remember everything I'd said.

"I think you should come down to the clinic on Monday. I can see if Clara can see you, or one of the other doctors," Everly said, clearly worried about me.

I sat back in the chair. "Fine."

"I think you need to talk to him, Bex," Poppy said. "Make sure it's really the way you think it is. Why don't you send him a text?" She nodded toward my phone.

With both their eyes on me, I picked up my phone

and typed a message, then hit send. Then I looked at them both and they smiled.

"We will find out exactly what is going on," she said, passing me the popcorn.

"It's going to be fine," Everly said. "It's probably not as bad as you think."

I shook my head, doubting their every word.

"We also slept together," I blurted.

Both girls looked over at me, shock on their faces.

"Alright, well, that just opened an entirely new can of worms."

CHAPTER NINE

Hudson

LIAM, Joe, and I all sat in my living room watching the game. I'd needed to be surrounded by my friends tonight. I needed to get out of my head. After listening to Bexley tell me her story, something inside of me snapped, and I was brought back to the horrific night I'd lived through years ago.

My phone vibrated in my pocket, and I grabbed it. I sighed when I saw Bexley's name on the screen. Never had I hated seeing her name as much as I did right now. Ignoring the message, I shut my phone off and shoved it back into my pocket.

"Come on!" Liam shouted, bringing me back to the living room.

"How the hell did he miss that?" Joe yelled.

"Where the hell are Tate and Dax?" Liam questioned, looking at his watch. "I knew I should have stopped and gotten the beer."

"They will be here. They sent a text ten minutes ago. Traffic."

I heard the slam of the front door and glanced at the boys. "There they are," I said, getting up and making my way to the door. I could use a beer right about now.

I rounded the corner, expecting to have a case of beer shoved my way, but was shocked when instead of Tate and Dax, Maya stood there.

"What the hell are you doing here?" I questioned, irritated that she was going to break up another guys' night out. I was also angry at her. She'd been the one who'd set this all up. She'd known my history.

"I need to talk to you," she said, not looking the least bit guilty.

"You need to talk to me? Why?" I barked.

"Please, Hudson. Bexley is a mess."

I rolled my eyes. "Well, it's a mess you created," I gritted. "You deal with it. I'm done."

Just then the door opened and in walked Tate and Dax, both laughing. The second they laid eyes on us, though, the laughter stopped. Dax handed me the case of beer, which I took into the kitchen and passed four bottles to Tate to carry into the living room for the guys. I took the moment to get some into the fridge when all I really wanted to do was to return and watch the game.

Maya took a couple of steps into the kitchen and leaned against the door. She said nothing; she just stood there watching me.

"Hudson, please."

"Please what?" I barked. "How the hell could you fix me up with her, knowing what she went through? Knowing full well that I could never be with someone who killed another person while they were driving?"

Maya knew the story well. I'd been friends with her brother when the accident happened.

"Come on, Hudson. Bex is nothing like the drunk driver who killed your pregnant girlfriend. There has to be more to the story than she is letting on. She was never arrested, and she was told it was an accident."

"Yeah, says you. You know, in my career, we have to accept the fact that sometimes there is just no justice for the victims who are completely innocent. This appears that it was one of those times. She got off. Lucky her."

"Come on, Hudson, you know Bex. Couldn't you see the way it tore her up when she told you?"

I chuckled in disbelief. "Yeah, just like I see it every day with the people who cause the accidents. Just like I saw in court when the lawyer got the guy off for taking away two people who meant the world to me. I see no difference here."

"You take that back."

I turned and met Maya's eyes. "I won't. She was lucky, and some poor girl out there is without the love of her life because of her."

"Does Bexley seem like someone who is irresponsible? Someone who would get behind the wheel of a car intoxicated just because?" Maya questioned, not once backing down.

Just then, Joe came into the kitchen. At first, I saw shock on his face at the fact his sister was here, but then he noticed the tension in the room. "What's going on?" he asked. "I could hear yelling all the way down the hall."

"Nothing!" we both shouted.

"Doesn't appear that way."

The room was so quiet you could have heard a pin drop. Joe stood there staring at the pair of us, probably not sure he should leave for fear one of us took a swing at the other. Finally, I ripped my eyes from hers. She had no idea the wound she'd opened by doing this. I turned to Joe.

"Did you know your sister fixed me up with someone who killed someone while driving? Someone who got off. Remind you of anything?"

Joe immediately turned to Maya. "What is he talking about?"

Maya turned away from me and crossed her arms. She shook her head. "Nothing."

"No way, doesn't sound like nothing. You better tell me what the hell is going on here, Maya."

She didn't turn around to face him. She just started talking.

"Bexley was involved in an accident on her way home in February. She hit someone, and they died. I guess she told Hudson about it, and now he is acting like she is just like the guy who killed his girlfriend all those years ago," she said, whipping around and glaring at me.

Joe looked at me, sadness coming over his face.

"I tried to tell him that this situation isn't the same, but he won't believe me."

Joe stepped between us, turned her around, and led her out into the hall. Then he turned to me. "I'll be right back," he muttered.

Moments later, he returned alone and leaned against the doorway. He said nothing, because really there was nothing to say. He'd been there with me through the entire trial. I knew he knew how I felt about this sort of stuff.

"I think you need to think this through. Take a minute and really look at this situation," he said quietly.

Joe probably knew me the best. He knew me well

enough to know I'd already slept with her; he knew me well enough to know I already had feelings for her. I knew that was why he was giving the advice he was giving. I walked to the door and slipped on my shoes.

"Where are you going?" Joe asked.

"I'm not sure. I think I just need to be alone for a while."

I SAT behind my desk at work. The office was quiet. It was the only place I could think of to go that no one would bother me. I'd hit the gym and then made my way to my desk. I'd logged into the computer and had sat with my fingers on the keyboard for a few minutes, debating if I should look up the accident Bexley had been involved in. It had been eating at me for hours, why she hadn't been charged. I knew I couldn't decide on the status of our relationship without knowing the truth.

I sat there thinking about us. I knew in my heart that I liked the idea of there being an us. I had to know the truth. It was the only way. The second the office was empty, I typed in the accident's date and her name to see if anything came up. Sure enough, a file appeared, so I began reading.

I heard a noise behind me and then felt a hand on my shoulder. I tore my eyes from the screen in front of me and looked up to see my boys. They grabbed chairs from other desks and sat down.

"So. You came to hide out here," Joe muttered.

"Who the hell comes to work on his day off?" Tate questioned, while Liam and Dax laughed.

"You doing okay?"

I nodded as I looked back at the screen.

"I feel like an ass."

"Why?" Joe asked. "Your feelings are valid. Maya should have known better, and had I have known about the situation beforehand, I'd have set her straight."

"No need. Maya was right. It was nothing like what happened with Carrie."

Joe frowned. "How do you know?"

I shrugged. "It was killing me, so I looked into it."

Joe ran his hand over his face. "What did you find out?"

"The guy she hit had a history with mental illness. Apparently, the girlfriend, who Bexley said was at the scene, reported he'd come off his meds a few months prior. She'd broke it off with him earlier that week when they'd been out for dinner because he was so erratic and dangerous. He'd called her that night from the side of the road, and when she got there, he threatened that if she didn't take him back, he'd walk out in front of the next car that came by. Which is what he did. It wasn't her fault at all. He literally walked out in front of her car, and she'd had no time to react. In the report, it said the officer told her that, and told her she wouldn't be charged. They called a friend of hers to come and get her, which I'm assuming was Maya."

"Wow."

"Like I say, I feel like an absolute dick for the way I left her."

"What do you mean?" Joe questioned.

I thought back to how things had gone the night before. To the sex we'd had and how, for the first time in years, I could see a relationship going somewhere. Then how only a few short hours later, I allowed those feelings from my experience to ruin things.

I looked at my best friends. "You let this slip to your sister and I'm going to come for you."

Liam looked over at Joe, I'm sure, fearing the worst.

"We slept together the night before, and when she shared part of something that was literally—and I mean literally—eating her alive, I bolted. No words, no explanation, no kiss goodbye, nothing. I was and am a complete ass."

CHAPTER TEN

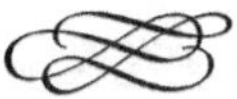

Bexley

I ROLLED over and smacked the alarm clock, silencing it. I'd just come off my last night shift and was feeling permanently drained. I didn't want to get up, yet I had to. I rolled onto my back and lay there, staring up at the ceiling.

It had been days since I'd heard from Hudson. I thought he would have messaged me during work, but he hadn't. I'd at least thought of him and had picked up my phone many times. I'd carefully typed out a message, but instead of hitting send, I deleted them. It wasn't exactly how Everly and I had talked about the messages going, so I'd not mentioned anything to her when she asked.

Besides, he still hadn't responded to the first one I'd sent when the girls were with me.

I hadn't heard from Maya either, which I found odd. Well, that was until I was on the bus this morning, coming home from the hospital. Days were getting shorter, so I'd started taking the bus again. She'd texted to see if I wanted to come to her place instead of doing our usual brunch day.

I'd given it some thought and responded with a yes once I'd gotten home. I had to move on. I couldn't continue to mope around the house, according to Clara, who I'd seen twice already this week.

I kicked the covers off and sat up, reaching for Hudson's sweater. Yes, I still had it, and yes, I wore it every chance I got. Even I was tiring of myself.

Poppy was picking me up in half an hour, so I quickly showered and dressed and made my way downstairs. I'd exited the elevator just in time to see her pull up.

We arrived at Maya's just in time for the sushi to arrive, and we all sat in her parents' dining room stuffing our faces and laughing.

I'd been amazed that Maya hadn't jumped on me the second I'd walked through the door. Instead, it was just like old times.

"I can't eat another bite," Everly said, shoving her plate away.

"Oh god I can," I muttered, grabbing more rolls and some sashimi from the tray. I had had little of an appetite over the past week, so I was making up for lost food.

"Have mine."

We all laughed while Poppy and Maya both dug into the tray again as well.

"We told you to go slow on those hand rolls." Poppy laughed, while Everly reached down and undid the button of her jeans.

"You better save room. We brought double fudge ice cream," Poppy added.

"Oh, tell me you didn't."

I couldn't help but laugh. We'd tortured her with that flavour, being it was her favourite.

"I'm going to weigh a thousand pounds after tonight," Everly whined.

"Me too," I added, "and you know what, I don't feel bad about it either." I shoved another piece of the volcano roll into my mouth.

We ate until we could eat no more, then cleaned up the table before making our way into the living room to start the movie. We'd all just sat down when the front door opened. I turned, expecting to see Maya's parents coming home from their card game. Instead, Joe, Liam, Dax, and Tate walked in followed by Hudson. The instant our eyes met, I turned away and pulled my phone from my pocket, trying to busy myself.

No one questioned why the guys were here, so that told me it had been planned.

"I think I'm going to go," I whispered to Everly.

She put her hand on mine and shook her head. "Don't leave."

It was then that the guys loaded into the living room, and I felt more trapped than ever. I glanced over at Poppy, hoping she'd take my expression and offer to drive me home, but she didn't. Instead, Maya cleared her throat.

"I'm sure you can guess by now that this was planned."

I avoided her eyes. She'd been the creator of this mess, and by the looks of things, she was going to end it, too.

"Yeah, you're both fucking miserable as hell, so we thought we'd bring you two together so you could talk," Joe said, coming into the living room a little more.

I could feel my body heating. It was going to be impossible to stop the panic attack that was threatening to spill over and consume me. Instead of saying anything, I looked from Poppy to Everly to Maya, and then got up and took off for Maya's room.

With the door shut, I felt better. I was away from the confrontation, and somehow I brought myself down into my safe zone. I sat down on the edge of her bed, hoping and praying that they'd all leave and I could go back to being with my friends.

It was quiet downstairs, and I hoped that it had happened when I heard a knock on her bedroom door. I didn't want to answer it, but then I heard another knock.

"Come in," I muttered, getting up and making my way toward the window.

I hadn't even bothered to look and see who it was. I wasn't all that interested in speaking with anyone at the moment. Only when I felt a large hand on my arm did I turn around to see Hudson standing there.

"I'm not talk—"

He brought his finger to my lips to silence me. "Listen. We need to talk."

I shook my head, but he once again didn't listen. Instead, he grabbed my hand and brought me over to the bed, pulling me down beside him.

"You are hurting, and I made it worse. Way worse," he whispered.

Instantly, his words brought tears to my eyes. Having him leave that morning after I'd confessed the entire situation had gutted me. I knew how I felt about myself after the accident, and it was the main reason I had told no one, because I didn't want my friends to look at me the same way. It hadn't helped that we'd spent the night before being so intimate with one another, either.

"It was my fault. I killed him." I sobbed.

"No, you didn't," he whispered, pulling me against him, trying to comfort me.

"I did. I saw the look in your eyes after I told you about the accident. You thought it too."

"Bex, listen to me."

"Don't tell me you didn't think it," I said, pulling away and wiping the tears from my cheeks.

"I won't lie. At first, yes, I thought something horrible. Then I thought about it. I wanted to know exactly what happened, so I went to the office and looked into it."

"I bet you did. I bet now you really think I'm a horrible person." I sniffled. "They should have just charged me. Thrown the book at me."

"No, Bex, they did exactly what I would have expected. The man you hit had many mental health issues. He'd been in and out of treatment and had stopped taking his medications. It wasn't your fault. He intentionally stepped out in front of your car and left you no time to stop or avoid him."

I turned and looked at Hudson. He stood and took a step toward me, holding his hands out. I met his eyes as the tears fell from mine. I slipped my hands into his and let him pull me to him. He wrapped his arms around me, pressing a kiss to my temple.

"I'm sorry," he whispered. "Sorry, I jumped to conclusions."

I said nothing. I just cried into his chest.

"I hope you can find it in your heart to forgive me. I'd really like a chance with you, with us."

I looked up and met his eyes. I nodded. "I'd like that," I whispered.

Without a moment's hesitation, he brought his lips to mine, kissing me hard. "How about we head back to your place?" he said.

I slowly nodded, hugged him, and then together, hand-in-hand, we made our way downstairs and said good night to our friends.

CHAPTER ELEVEN

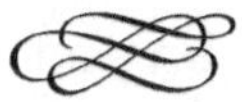

Hudson

WE LAY ON MY COUCH. The only light in the room came from the flickering candle that sat on the coffee table. I knew I had to tell her why I'd gotten so upset. Joe had told me there was no way our relationship was going to work if I wasn't open and honest with her. I just wasn't sure when or how to tell her.

We'd left Maya's parents' place and drove around town for a bit before parking down at the water's edge. We cuddled up together and sat on the tailgate of my truck and watched the fireworks the summer festival held on the last night. After, we walked barefoot along the beach, until Bexley admitted she had a headache. Since my place was closer, we came here instead of going to hers. We'd come in, I'd turned the lights off, and we'd curled up together on the couch. She rested her head on my chest while I held her in my arms.

"How you feeling?" I quietly asked.

"Better," she said, letting out a yawn. "I'm tired."

I glanced at the clock; it was already close to midnight, and while I hadn't planned on taking her home tonight, I figured maybe this was the hint she wanted to leave. It was then I heard Joe's voice again, urging me to talk to her. That had been the purpose of ambushing the girls' evening.

"Before I take you home, could we talk?" I asked.

She looked at me with disappointment in her eyes. Perhaps I'd read that hint wrong, too. Maybe she didn't want to go back home.

"Sure," she said, interlocking her fingers with mine. "What's on your mind?"

"I need to tell you something. I don't want it to start another argument. I think you need to know why I got so upset the other morning."

I felt her still, then prop herself up on her forearm. I could see just enough of her face from the flickering candle to know she was watching me, waiting for me to explain what had caused my outburst. "What is it?" she questioned.

When I didn't answer her, she rose up a little farther.

"Should I turn the light on?" she questioned, reaching for the lamp on the side table, but I stopped her.

"No, no," I said, grabbing her hand. "This is fine. Did I ever tell you about Carrie?"

She shook her head. "Don't think so."

"She was my girlfriend back in college."

She stilled again. "Is this where you are going to tell me she called you and wants you back? Oh god, did it happen right after we slept together?"

I shook my head, then pushed the hair that had fallen into her face away from her eyes. "No, nothing like that," I said.

Bexley was quiet. "Okay, I'm not sure what to think here."

I was quiet. Perhaps this was a shitty time to bring this up. We were on talking terms again, she was in my arms again. Maybe she didn't need to know, and to be honest, I wasn't good with this stuff. But Joe and the guys had told me I needed to tell her. I just wanted to get it out, so it was done and over with. I didn't want something else festering between us.

"She isn't my ex."

Bexley giggled. "This isn't getting better, Hudson," she said, going to sit up, but I stopped her.

"Just listen. I'm not good with this sort of stuff, and like you, I haven't told very many people about this," I whispered.

Bexley quieted down, rested her head on her hand and waited. "Take all the time you need."

"We didn't break up. We went out while we were in college. Prom night, like most relationships, we had sex. She got pregnant. Our parents were furious, but I was so happy, I didn't even care. We'd both graduated, and I had jobs lined up. So I planned to do what any man would do. I was going to marry her, and we were going to raise that baby."

"Okay."

"Only, I never got the chance."

"What happened? Did her parents not like that you were taking the responsible approach? Did they take her from you, or make her have an abortion?"

I swallowed hard and stared at the ceiling.

"She was on her way home one night from work. She had to take a detour because of construction and was hit head on by a drunk driver."

"Oh, my god." Bexley gasped. "How awful."

"When you told me about your accident, and said you weren't charged, it triggered me. See, the driver who hit Carrie got off on a technicality. It literally ate me alive, knowing that this guy would not be punished for what he had taken from me. Which was what I thought happened with your accident. Even though I knew you hadn't been drinking, you'd still taken someone away from someone else. Like you, he didn't even have a scratch on him. I lost her and our unborn child, and he got off. It brought back to all these horrid memories, all those feelings of what I'd lost."

Bexley said nothing. She just watched me, waiting for me to say more.

"Her accident is the reason I fight so hard to put drunk drivers and the people who cause the accidents behind bars, or at least keep them off the streets. It wasn't the fact you'd hit the guy. The trigger happened when you told me you'd gotten off."

"I can understand that."

"I just want you to know I'm sorry. I was wrong to assume the things I did."

"Shhh, no need to be sorry."

"No, there is. I treated you terribly. Not the way I should have treated you the morning after our first time. I'll never be able to let that go or forgive myself."

Bexley pressed her lips to mine. "Thank you for trusting me with that," she said, kissing me again. "As for the second part, you can make that up to me."

She climbed over me, and once standing, she took hold of my hand and gently tugged.

"Did you want to go home?" I questioned, getting up off the couch and wrapping my arm around her waist.

She shook her head, turned to face me. "I think it's time we go make up," she said pressing her lips to mine.

CHAPTER TWELVE

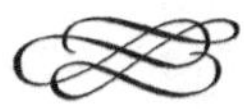

Bexley - Six weeks later

IT WAS dark as I crossed the parking lot of the hospital. I could see the fireflies dancing in the bushes beside my parked car, and I smiled to myself. I'd always loved those weird little bugs.

I'd just gotten into my car and attached my phone to my charger when my phone rang. I hit the answer button on my steering wheel.

"Hey."

"Hey, sweetie. How was your shift?"

I let out a yawn, excited to hear Hudson's voice. He'd been away at a conference the last week, and with my schedule, we hadn't been able to chat for very long.

"Busy. I'm actually pretty exhausted tonight."

"How have you been making out driving in the dark?" he questioned.

I'd asked him to help me regain some control over that part of my life, and so far, he'd done nothing but encourage me. He'd come up with a plan and so far it had been working fine.

"Okay, so far. I took the bus last night, though, and left my car in the parking lot," I answered, taking a sip of the coffee I'd gotten from the cafeteria before getting in the car.

"One day at a time. No need to stress yourself out. You going to come by later?" he asked, yawning.

I looked at the clock. He was just starting his night shift as I was ending mine. I'd honestly been hoping to see him tonight. I'd planned to just go to his place and surprise him, until he'd messaged to say he had to go into work.

"How about you come by my place when you're done with your shift?"

"I think I could do that."

"Maybe you could bring your handcuffs too?" I said, feeling my cheeks heat as I bit my bottom lip.

He chuckled, and that was when I heard his car door slam. "Another booty call?" I heard Joe ask in the background.

"Oh my god, please tell me he didn't hear that?" I said, my face surely completely red at this point.

Hudson chuckled again. "Relax, he heard nothing, sweetie. How about you message me once you get home so I know you are safe?"

"Will do. Love you."

"Love you too."

I hung up and secured my seat belt, then placed the brown paper bag I'd gotten from the pharmacy on the seat beside me. A wave of nausea hit me as I wondered what the results would be.

I LAY IN BED, staring at the ceiling. I hadn't slept all night. Instead, I'd tossed and turned, fighting every single thought in my mind. I glanced at the clock. It was a little after seven, and I knew any minute I'd hear Hudson's key in the lock. Sure enough, two minutes later, I heard exactly that.

I rolled onto my side, fighting off another wave of nausea, when I heard the bedroom door open. He said nothing, which meant he thought I was asleep. I closed my eyes, listening as he undressed, then I felt the mattress dip down. In a matter of moments, his arm wrapped around my waist and he pressed a kiss on my shoulder.

"You awake?" he whispered. "I brought what you asked me to bring."

I felt the chill of the cold steel against my wrist and jumped.

"Fuck I thought you were asleep," he said.

"Sorry, that was damn cold. You could have warmed them up a little first," I said, laughing.

He grabbed me, rolled me onto my back, and pressed his lips to mine, sliding his hand under my shirt and gently passing his fingers over my hardened nipples while kissing the side of my neck.

It was a matter of minutes before the cold steel of that handcuff secured my hands to the headboard and Hudson was so deep inside of me all I could do was moan.

He held onto my hip with one hand, the other in my hair, ever so gently tugging every once in a while.

"God, I love taking you like this." He groaned as his body stiffened and he poured himself into me.

He got off the bed and, grabbing his keys, he quickly undid the cuffs and then smacked me on the ass as he left the room. He came back with a hot cloth and cleaned me up, before sliding back into bed and pulling me into his arms.

"My god, I can't believe that Everly is pregnant," Hudson said, pulling into his driveway and cutting the engine of his truck.

"I know, but did you see how happy they were?" I said, thinking back to their announcement at dinner tonight. "I'm so happy for them. Maya was a little shocked. I wonder how her parents are going to take the news."

"They haven't told them yet?" Hudson questioned.

"Not that Maya told me. I don't know. Maybe they were testing it out on us first." I giggled.

"Perhaps we should have pulled the parent routine, so they had practice." Hudson chuckled, climbing out of the truck.

I climbed out of the truck and followed him inside his house, wondering all the way how I was going to break the news to him I too was pregnant. I'd taken the test I'd gotten from the pharmacy shortly before we'd left for dinner, and took the second one just to be sure. I'd even booked an appointment with an OBGYN from the hospital before he'd picked me up.

"I'm not sure we'd play the part correctly. I don't

think I've ever seen Joe and Maya's parents get really angry at anything."

"I have. Trust me, it's not pretty." Hudson chuckled.

"Well, they are living together. I'd imagine it would be worse if it were Maya and Liam."

"Oh god, could you imagine. They've been sneaking around for months, too, and under their roof. That I'd love to be a fly on the wall for."

I laughed, thinking back to Maya telling us how her parents had demanded there be no sex under their roof. I could only imagine the fallout.

"They looked pretty excited, though," Hudson said as he walked into the living room with two glasses of wine. "For you," he said, holding the glass for me to take.

I did so, but didn't drink it. Instead, I placed it on the table and smiled up at him.

"Well, that is a first that you didn't drink that puppy down. It is your favourite, just so you know. I'm done trying to get you to drink the drier stuff." He winked, sitting down beside me.

"It's not that," I said.

"Just not in the mood for wine tonight?" he asked, brushing the strands of hair that were covering my eyes.

I shook my head, meeting his eyes. "I'd actually kill for a glass right about now."

"So...drink up." He took a mouthful of his wine. Then, as if it hit him, he stopped, lowered the glass, and looked over at me. "What…what are you…saying?" he mumbled, looking at me with hopeful eyes.

I nodded. "I'm pregnant."

Hudson sat forward, placing his glass on the table, and placed a kiss on my lips before wrapping his arms around me and pulling me in for a hug. "You're sure?"

"I'm pretty sure. I have an appointment with the doctor next week to confirm, but two tests told me yes."

I could already see the excitement in his eyes and knew that he was happy about this news. I didn't need to worry about that. He hugged me again and then chuckled to himself as he picked up my glass of wine and poured it into his. "Sorry for teasing you with this."

"You didn't know," I answered.

"No, but I should have known something was up when all you did was stick to water for dinner. Even the girls wondered about that."

I couldn't help but smile. "Are you excited?"

"Hell ya, I am. Fuck, I wish you'd have said something earlier. We could have blown Joe and Everly's announcement out of the water."

"Oh, believe me, I think it will when the time is right to announce this to our friends."

"I think you are right." Hudson laughed, pulling me in for another hug.

I LAY ON MY SIDE, wrapped in Hudson's arms, still sweaty and breathing hard. We'd taken the night to talk about the future and had decided that in the next few weeks, I'd be moving in with him. He'd already marked down the first doctor's appointment in his calendar and had already messaged Dax to see if he could cover for him at work that afternoon. Of course, I'd laughed at Hudson's reaction when Dax was full of questions. I'd also threatened to cut Hudson off if he even hinted at why he needed him to cover for him.

He pressed his lips against the back of my neck as he pulled me tighter against him. "You're sure you're happy about this?" I questioned, knowing full well what the answer was already.

"Don't even go there," he whispered. "I'll have to break out the handcuffs again."

"Yes, please." I giggled.

I was so excited about what the future held. I was with a great man, one I'd never even considered being a significant other if it hadn't been for Maya. I was so glad that things hadn't ended when they could have.

I rolled over in his arms and looked into his eyes.

"Would it be silly if I told you I can't wait to meet him or her?" I questioned.

He softly smiled. "No, not at all."

He pressed a kiss to my lips, and I closed my eyes and nestled myself against his chest. Laying in his warm arms would forever be my favorite thing.

As I lay there, I thought of all the things over the last couple of months I had to be thankful for. First, I would forever be thankful to my best friend for giving me this opportunity, even if at the time I was less than thrilled, and to my other best friends for making me think twice and forcing me to hear him out before ending everything.

I'd always think back to these summer nights when I'd fallen in love and to those fireflies I saw the morning I'd purchased those tests before coming home, and I'd forever love the man who gave me this life that was growing inside of me.

GET TWO FREE BOOKS

Sign up for my newsletter and I'll send you two FREE books.

https://geni.us/NLSignupBackMatter

Follow S.L. Sterling

Did you know that bookbub has a feature where you can follow me and it will send you an alert when I release a book or put a title on sale? Sign up here and make sure you stay in the loop.

Bookbub:
https://geni.us/SLSterlingBookbub

Website
https://www.authorslsterling.com

Facebook
https://geni.us/SLSterlingFB

Instagram
https://geni.us/SLSterlingInstagram

Tiktok
https://geni.us/slsterlingtiktok

Reader Group
https://geni.us/SapphiresReaderGroup

Goodreads
https://geni.us/SterlingGoodreads

Newsletter
https://geni.us/NLSignupBackMatter

ABOUT THE AUTHOR

USA Today Bestselling Author S.L. Sterling was born and raised in southern Ontario.

An avid reader all her life, S.L. Sterling dreamt of becoming an author. She decided to give writing a try after one of her favorite authors launched a course on how to write your novel. This course gave her the push she needed to put pen to paper and her debut novel "It Was Always You" was born.

When S.L. Sterling isn't writing or plotting her next

novel she can be found curled up with a cup of coffee, blanket and the newest romance novel from one of her favorite authors.

In her spare time, she enjoys camping, hiking, sunny destinations, spending quality time with family and friends and of course reading.

OTHER BOOKS BY S.L. STERLING

It Was Always You

On A Silent Night

Bad Company

Back to You this Christmas

Fireside Love

Holiday Wishes

Saviour Boy

The Boy Under the Gazebo

The Greatest Gift

Into the Sunset

Letting You Go

The Spencer Brooks Diaries

Our Little Secret

Our Little Surprise

Our Little Wedding

The Malone Brother Series
A Kiss Beneath the Stars
In Your Arms
His to Hold
Finding Forever with You

Vegas MMA
Dagger

Doctors of Eastport General
Doctor Desire
Doctor Right
Doctor Frost

All I Want for Christmas (Contemporary Romance Holiday Collection)

Willow Valley
Memories of the Past
To Trust my Heart
Letters from the Heart
What Once Was Broken
Scars on my Heart

The Happy Holidates Series

Pop Tarts and Mistletoe
Champagne and Fireworks
Summer Nights and Fireflies

Vancouver Dominators
Inside the Penalty Box
Ten Minute Misconduct
Crossing the Red Line
Two Minutes for Holding
Playing the Neutral Zone
Through the Five Hole

9 781998 649235